致敬译界巨匠许渊冲先生

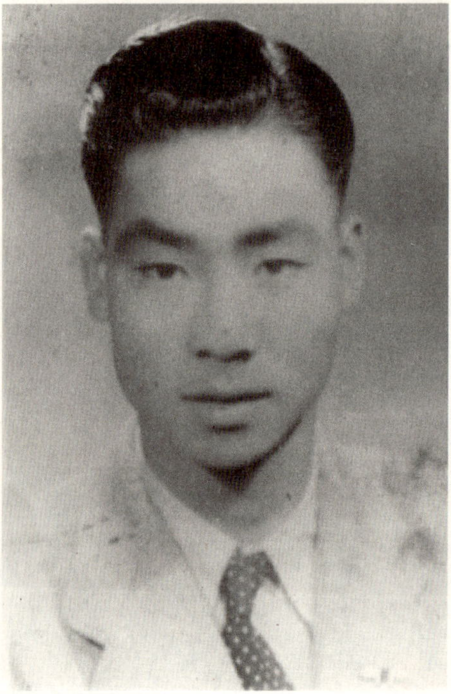

许渊冲译
唐宋词一百首
100 TANG AND SONG LYRICS

选译

中国出版集团
中译出版社

目录
Contents

| 译 序

002	[唐] 无名氏 Anonymous	鹊踏枝 Tune: The Magpie on a Branch
004	[唐] 无名氏 Anonymous	摊破浣溪沙 Tune: Broken Form of Sand of Silk-washing Stream
006	[唐] 李　白 Li Bai	菩萨蛮 Tune: Buddhist Dancers
008	[唐] 李　白 Li Bai	忆秦娥 Tune: Dream of a Maid of Honour
010	[唐] 白居易 Bai Juyi	长相思 Tune: Everlasting Longing
012	[唐] 张志和 Zhang Zhihe	渔歌子 Tune: A Fisherman's Song
014	[唐] 刘禹锡 Liu Yuxi	竹枝词 Tune: Bamboo Branch Song
016	[唐] 刘禹锡 Liu Yuxi	浪淘沙 Tune: Ripples Sifting Sand
018	[唐] 温庭筠 Wen Tingyun	梦江南 Tune: Dreaming of the South
020	[唐] 温庭筠 Wen Tingyun	河传 Tune: From the River
022	[唐] 皇甫松 Huangfu Song	忆江南 Tune: The South Recalled
024	[唐] 韦　庄 Wei Zhuang	菩萨蛮 Tune: Buddhist Dancers

026	[唐]李 珣	南乡子	
	Li Xun	Tune: Song of a Southern Country	
028	[唐]孙光宪	酒泉子	
	Sun Guangxian	Tune: Fountain of Wine	
030	[南唐]冯延巳	谒金门	
	Feng Yansi	Tune: Paying Homage at the Golden Gate	
032	[南唐]李 煜	破阵子	
	Li Yu	Tune: Dance of the Cavalry	
034	[南唐]李 煜	相见欢	
	Li Yu	Tune: Joy at Meeting	
036	[南唐]李 煜	乌夜啼	
	Li Yu	Tune: Crows Crying at Night	
038	[南唐]李 煜	浪淘沙	
	Li Yu	Tune: Ripples Sifting Sand	
040	[南唐]李 煜	虞美人	
	Li Yu	Tune: The Beautiful Lady Yu	
042	[宋]林 逋	长相思	
	Lin Bu	Tune: Everlasting Longing	
044	[宋]潘 阆	酒泉子	
	Pan Lang	Tune: Fountain of Wine	
046	[宋]柳 永	昼夜乐	
	Liu Yong	Tune: Joy of Day and Night	
048	[宋]柳 永	雨霖铃	
	Liu Yong	Tune: Bells Ringing in the Rain	
052	[宋]柳 永	望海潮	
	Liu Yong	Tune: Watching the Tidal Bore	
056	[宋]柳 永	八声甘州	
	Liu Yong	Tune: Eight Beats of a Ganzhou Song	

060	[宋] 范仲淹 Fan Zhongyan	渔家傲 Tune: Pride of Fishermen	
062	[宋] 范仲淹 Fan Zhongyan	苏幕遮 Tune: Screened by Southern Curtain	
064	[宋] 张　先 Zhang Xian	玉楼春 Tune: Spring in Jade Pavilion	
066	[宋] 晏　殊 Yan Shu	浣溪沙 Tune: Sand of Silk-washing Stream	
068	[宋] 晏　殊 Yan Shu	破阵子 Tune: Dance of the Cavalry	
070	[宋] 张　昪 Zhang Bian	离亭燕 Tune: Swallows Leaving Pavilion	
072	[宋] 欧阳修 Ouyang Xiu	生查子 Tune: Mountain Hawthorn	
074	[宋] 欧阳修 Ouyang Xiu	蝶恋花 Tune: Butterflies Lingering over Flowers	
076	[宋] 王安石 Wang Anshi	桂枝香 Tune: Fragrance of Laurel Branch	
080	[宋] 王安石 Wang Anshi	南乡子 Tune: Song of a Southern Country	
082	[宋] 王　观 Wang Guan	卜算子 Tune: Song of Divination	
084	[宋] 苏　轼 Su Shi	虞美人 Tune: The Beautiful Lady Yu	
086	[宋] 苏　轼 Su Shi	江城子 Tune: A Riverside Town	
088	[宋] 苏　轼 Su Shi	江城子 Tune: A Riverside Town	

090	[宋] 苏　轼 Su Shi	水调歌头 Tune: Prelude to the Melody of water	
094	[宋] 苏　轼 Su Shi	浣溪沙 Tune: Sand of Silk-washing Stream	
096	[宋] 苏　轼 Su Shi	浣溪沙 Tune: Sand of Silk-washing Stream	
098	[宋] 苏　轼 Su Shi	永遇乐 Tune: Joy of Eternal Union	
102	[宋] 苏　轼 Su Shi	西江月 Tune: The Moon over the West River	
104	[宋] 苏　轼 Su Shi	定风波 Tune: Calming the Waves	
106	[宋] 苏　轼 Su Shi	念奴娇 Tune: Charm of a Maiden Singer	
110	[宋] 苏　轼 Su Shi	临江仙 Tune: Immortal at the River	
112	[宋] 苏　轼 Su Shi	水龙吟 Tune: Water Dragon Chant	
116	[宋] 苏　轼 Su Shi	蝶恋花 Tune: Butterflies Lingering over Flowers	
118	[宋] 李之仪 Li Zhiyi	卜算子 Tune: Song of Divination	
120	[宋] 黄庭坚 Huang Tingjian	清平乐 Tune: Pure Serene Music	
122	[宋] 秦　观 Qin Guan	鹊桥仙 Tune: Immortal at the Magpie Bridge	
124	[宋] 秦　观 Qin Guan	踏莎行 Tune: Treading on Grass	

126	[宋] 贺　铸 He Zhu	捣练子 Tune: Song of Broken Chains
128	[宋] 贺　铸 He Zhu	鹧鸪天 Tune: The Partridge Sky
130	[宋] 周邦彦 Zhou Bangyan	苏幕遮 Tune: Screened by Southern Curtain
132	[宋] 周邦彦 Zhou Bangyan	蝶恋花 Tune: Butterflies Lingering over Flowers
134	[宋] 朱敦儒 Zhu Dunru	相见欢 Tune: Joy at Meeting
136	[宋] 李清照 Li Qingzhao	如梦令 Tune: Like A Dream
138	[宋] 李清照 Li Qingzhao	一剪梅 Tune: A Twig of Mume Blossoms
140	[宋] 李清照 Li Qingzhao	醉花阴 Tune: Tipsy in the Flower's Shade
142	[宋] 李清照 Li Qingzhao	渔家傲 Tune: Pride of Fishermen
144	[宋] 李清照 Li Qingzhao	凤凰台上忆吹箫 Tune: Playing Flute Recalled on Phoenix Terrace
148	[宋] 李清照 Li Qingzhao	声声慢 Tune: Slow, Slow Tune
152	[宋] 李清照 Li Qingzhao	永遇乐 Tune: Joy of Eternal Union
156	[宋] 陈与义 Chen Yuyi	临江仙 Tune: Immortal at the River
158	[宋] 张元干 Zhang Yuangan	贺新郎 Tune: Congratulating the Bridegroom

162	[宋] 岳 飞 Yue Fei	满江红 Tune: The River All Red	
166	[宋] 岳 飞 Yue Fei	满江红 Tune: The River All Red	
170	[宋] 岳 飞 Yue Fei	小重山 Tune: Manifold Little Hill	
172	[宋] 陆 游 Lu You	钗头凤 Tune: Phoenix Hairpin	
176	[宋] 陆 游 Lu You	诉衷情 Tune: Telling of Innermost Feelings	
178	[宋] 陆 游 Lu You	卜算子 Tune: Song of Divination	
180	[宋] 张孝祥 Zhang Xiaoxiang	念奴娇 Tune: The Charm of A Maiden Singer	
184	[宋] 张孝祥 Zhang Xiaoxiang	西江月 Tune: The Moon over the West River	
186	[宋] 辛弃疾 Xin Qiji	水龙吟 Tune: Water Dragon Chant	
190	[宋] 辛弃疾 Xin Qiji	菩萨蛮 Tune: Buddhist Dancers	
192	[宋] 辛弃疾 Xin Qiji	摸鱼儿 Tune: Groping for Fish	
196	[宋] 辛弃疾 Xin Qiji	清平乐 Tune: Pure Serene Music	
198	[宋] 辛弃疾 Xin Qiji	清平乐 Tune: Pure Serene Music	
200	[宋] 辛弃疾 Xin Qiji	采桑子 Tune: Song of Picking Mulberry	

202	[宋] 辛弃疾 Xin Qiji	青玉案 Tune: Green Jade Cup
204	[宋] 辛弃疾 Xin Qiji	破阵子 Tune: Dance of the Cavalry
206	[宋] 辛弃疾 Xin Qiji	西江月 Tune: The Moon over the West River
208	[宋] 辛弃疾 Xin Qiji	西江月 Tune: The Moon over the West River
210	[宋] 辛弃疾 Xin Qiji	鹧鸪天 Tune: The Partridge Sky
212	[宋] 辛弃疾 Xin Qiji	永遇乐 Tune: Joy of Eternal Union
216	[宋] 辛弃疾 Xin Qiji	南乡子 Tune: Song of a Southern Country
218	[宋] 陈　亮 Chen Liang	水调歌头 Tune: Prelude to Water Melody
222	[宋] 刘　过 Liu Guo	西江月 Tune: The Moon over the West River
224	[宋] 姜　夔 Jiang Kui	扬州慢 Tune: Slow Tune of Yangzhou
228	[宋] 姜　夔 Jiang Kui	鹧鸪天 Tune: The Partridge Sky
230	[宋] 刘克庄 Liu Kezhuang	玉楼春 Tune: Spring in Jade Pavilion
232	[宋] 吴文英 Wu Wenying	八声甘州 Tune: Eight Beats of a Ganzhou Song
236	[宋] 吴文英 Wu Wenying	风入松 Tune: Wind through Pines

238	[宋] 刘辰翁 Liu Chenweng	柳梢青 Tune: Green Tip of Willow Branch
240	[宋] 文天祥 Wen Tianxiang	念奴娇 Tune: Charm of a Maiden Singer
244	[宋] 文天祥 Wen Tianxiang	沁园春 Tune: Spring in the Garden of Qin
248	[宋] 张 炎 Zhang Yan	清平乐 Tune: Pure Serene Music

译　序

《中国词选》罗马尼亚译者说："中国的词使我们认识了一个毋庸置疑的充满魅力、抒情性强和意境深邃的世界，在这个世界里洋溢着书面上看到的花朵的香气"，中国的词"是三千多年悠久文化与文明的结晶"[①]。

我国词的兴起，可以追溯到隋代。著名的《河传》《柳枝》就是当时的民歌，《水调》也是开凿运河的产物。到了唐代，词有了新的发展。1900年在敦煌发现的唐人曲词残卷，共有1160余首，其中多数来自民间，有鲜明的性格特征和浓厚的生活气息，如《菩萨蛮》：

枕前发尽千般愿，要休且待青山烂。
水面上秤锤浮，直待黄河彻底枯。
白日参辰现，北斗回南面。
休即未能休，且待三更见日头！

这首词写爱情的盟誓，充满了坚贞的信念，火一样的热

[①] 转引自1981年2月1日《人民日报》。

情,新颖泼辣,奇特生动。就形式而言,第三句中的"上"字和第四句、第八句中的"直待""且待",都是衬字。如果把衬字取消,形式就和其他《菩萨蛮》的曲调一致了。此外,《菩萨蛮》的调名也说明了佛教对唐代文化的影响。

这本词集里选了两首唐代民间词,第一首《鹊踏枝》通过妇人和灵鹊的对话,写出了妇人对和平幸福生活的热烈向往,表现手法相当新颖灵活,语言也活泼生动。此外,《鹊踏枝》的调名也说明了词的内容和调名最初是有关系的。

文人词里最早的作品,据说是李白的《菩萨蛮》和《忆秦娥》,但也有人认为这两首词都是后来无名词人写的。《菩萨蛮》一词据说"写在鼎州沧水驿楼","解者或依此,以为既写在驿楼,当即在驿楼中所作。既驿楼中作,当即为男子自己抒怀乡之情,故定此词的主人公是男子"[1]。但是靳极苍说:"就词本身来看,还是解作闺情,定主人公为怀远盼归的少妇为好。"我在这里译成"闺情"。

《忆秦娥》一词,靳极苍说:"作者借秦娥的忆旧,以抒发自己伤逝的感情。"李汉超却在《论李白〈忆秦娥〉》[2]一文中认为这词是"一首以天宝之乱为背景、充满政治激情的反映唐代由盛转衰的伤时之作"。加上《忆秦娥》的调名与词的内容有关,可能是最初的作品,因此他认为这词不是后人的伪作。我觉得他的话很有道理,也在英文注释中做了说明。

唐代文人的理想,不是在朝为官,就是在野为民,过隐居的渔樵生活。这种理想反映在词中的,有张志和的《渔歌子》。这首词的内容和调名一致,被誉为"风流千古",在

---

[1] 见靳极苍《唐宋词百首详解》。
[2] 见《文学评论》1983年第4期。

当时影响很大，和者如林，很快就传到了日本。据《日本填词学史话》的记载：嵯峨天皇（804—823年在位）还曾亲和了五首。

后来，刘禹锡、白居易也相继作词。刘禹锡模仿四川民歌，写了一组有名的《竹枝词》。这里选译了他的一首《竹枝词》和一首《浪淘沙》。《浪淘沙》写妇女结伴到沙滩淘金，内容和调名相关，形式却与后来的《浪淘沙》不同，反而跟七言绝句相近。由此也可看出：词体的形成实际上源自民歌和绝句[①]。经过刘、白等文人提倡，词逐渐从民间文学的地位登上了文坛。

到了晚唐，涌现出了一批以填词为主要表现手段的艺术家，其中以皇甫松、温庭筠等最为著名。温庭筠作品比较多，词的形式格律到他手里才逐渐完善起来。温庭筠改变了民间词朴素的风格，特别注重修辞的华丽。如《更漏子》：

柳丝长，春雨细，花外漏声迢递。
惊塞雁，起城乌，画屏金鹧鸪。
香雾薄，透帘幕，惆怅谢家池阁。
红烛背，绣帘垂，梦长君不知。

这是一首描写深夜失眠的妇女思念情人的词，写得隐微曲折，婉约含蓄，不好翻译。这里只选译了一首《梦江南》，其中"一切景语"都是"情语"。

温庭筠是"花间派"的代表作家，韦庄和温庭筠齐名，并称"温韦"。温庭筠的风格和李商隐相近，韦庄的风格和

---

① 据周永济《唐五代两宋词简析》总论。

白居易相近。韦词浅显如话，富有民间气息，例如他追念为王建夺去的宠姬而作的《女冠士》：

四月十七，正是去年今日。
别君时，忍泪佯低面，含羞半敛眉。
不知魂已断，空有梦相随。
除却天边月，没人知。

夏承焘认为韦庄词的最大特点，"是把当时文人词带回到民间作品的抒情道路上来"，"影响了后来的李煜、苏轼、辛弃疾诸大家"。①

其他"花间派"的词人，夏承焘认为他们共同的特点是："华丽的字面，婉约的表达手法，集中来写女性的美貌和服饰以及她们的离愁别恨。"这里选译了两首风格不同的词：一首是李珣所写的具有浓厚南方乡土色彩的《南乡子》；一首是孙光宪刻画塞外荒凉图景的《酒泉子》。

"花间派"的作者大都是西蜀词人。在晚唐五代与西蜀词并峙的，还有长江下游的另一个词派——南唐词。冯延巳与韦庄分据吴蜀词坛。冯词"所以娱宾而遣兴也"②，对北宋词坛影响很大。刘熙载《艺概》中说："冯延巳词，晏同叔（晏殊）得其俊，欧阳永叔（欧阳修）得其深。"冯词和欧词风格近似，有时难分彼此，如这里选译的《蝶恋花》"庭院深深"一词，就既见于冯词集，又见于欧词集。"庭院深深"，夏承焘说是指一个贵族少妇的深闺，靳极苍却说是指"歌

---

① 见夏承焘《唐宋词欣赏》。
② 见陈世修为冯延巳《阳春集》作的序。

楼妓馆"，译文按照靳说更合逻辑。

　　五代词的代表作家，是南唐后主李煜。"李煜词改革'花间派'涂饰、雕琢的流弊，用清丽的语言、白描的手法和高度的艺术概括力，抓住自己生活感受中最深刻的方面，动人地把情感表达出来，给人深刻的艺术感受"。[1]王国维在《人间词话》中说："温飞卿（温庭筠）之词，句秀也；韦端己（韦庄）之词，骨秀也；李重光（李煜）之词，神秀也。词至李后主而眼界始大，感慨遂深，遂变伶工之词而为士大夫之词。"又说："词人者，不失其赤子之心者也。故生于深宫之中，长于妇人之手，是后主为人君所短处，亦即为词人所长处。客观之诗人不可不多阅世，阅世愈深则材料愈丰富，愈变化，《水浒传》《红楼梦》之作者是也。主观之诗人不必多阅世，阅世愈浅则性情愈真，李后主是也。尼采谓一切文学，余爱以血书者。后主之词。真所谓以血书者也。"这里选译了李煜词五首，其中《乌夜啼》一首，美国耶鲁大学"词学"教授孙康宜认为词人把"春红""寒雨"和"胭脂泪"相比，有独到见解，我的译文采用了孙说。

　　北宋早期的词家中，潘阆以狂放不羁著称。他所作的《酒泉子》（《忆余杭》）最享盛名，苏轼亲手书于玉堂屏风之上，石曼卿也使画师为之绘图，这里选译了其中一首。林逋是妻梅子鹤的高士，这里选译了他的一首《长相思》。

　　北宋早期独放异彩的词人是范仲淹。他的词作不多，却是字字珠玉。这里选译了他的《渔家傲》和《苏幕遮》，前者苍凉悲壮，后者缠绵悱恻，"字号见性情、见抱负，真是佳作。这些词能于温婉之中寓豪宕之气，对于后世豪放词派

[1] 见夏承焘《唐宋词欣赏》。

V

的兴起，是有影响的"。[1]

北宋词林的早期领袖人物是晏殊和欧阳修。晏殊是个神童，年仅十四，就赐同进士出身，成为一代名相。他的词作"清新含蓄"[2]，名句如"无可奈何花落去，似曾相识燕归来"，属对工巧，自然而又深挚地表现了主人公惜春的心绪，为世盛称。

欧阳修是北宋古文运动的领袖，他的诗文风骨峻肃，词却显浅轻快侧艳。这里选译了他的《生查子》和《蝶恋花》，前者一说是朱淑贞所作，后者一说是冯延巳的词。

北宋前期的词以小令为主，基本上没有超出南唐五代的婉约词风，然而较以前更加雍容秀雅。"把短小纤巧的小令发展成为繁音缛节、局面开张的慢词，是柳永的一大贡献。"[3] 柳永是北宋第一个专业词人，周笃文认为他对词有四个贡献："第一，发展了词体。""第二，扩大了词境。如表现都市繁华、山川壮丽的《望海潮》。""第三，对下层人民的同情。""第四，技巧的发展。长于铺叙，惯用白描手法，以'到口即消'的通俗语言传情状物，这是柳词艺术上的主要长处。比如《八声甘州》。"

柳永的代表作是《雨霖铃》。詹安泰在《宋词散论》中说："这是描写他要离开汴京（开封）去各地漂泊时和他心爱的人难舍难分的痛苦心情。""这首词的上半阕主要是写临别时的情景，下半阕主要是写别后的情景。"唐圭璋等编的《唐宋词选注》，夏承焘等编的《唐宋词选》，刘永济的《唐五代两宋词简析》，解释都差不多，都"认为是写别情的典范

[1] 见周笃文《宋词》。
[2] 见詹安泰《宋词散论》。
[3] 见周笃文《宋词》。下同。

之作"。但是靳极苍在《唐宋词百首详解》中却说:"这首词是描写一个妇女在暮秋送别时的惜别情况"。《语文教学与研究》1983年第7期中也说:"词的上阕是写她和情侣执手握别的感受,下阕是写她握别后独守空房的心情。上阕的场景在室外、在长亭,下阕的场景在室内、在空房。上阕写两情相对,下阕写两情天各一方。"说法也有道理。但是英文已按詹说译好,修改会牵一发而动全身,只好作罢。

北宋前期词人还有张先和王安石。张先的佳作如"云破月来花弄影""无数杨花过无影"等,都是脍炙人口的名句,因此他有"张三影"的雅号。王安石曾任北宋宰相,创行新法,力革弊政。他的《桂枝香》词,上片写山川形势,气象开阔;下片转入人事,着重指出竞逐繁华乃是六朝相继败亡的原因,被推为登临的绝唱。

继晏、欧、柳永之后,大拓词境、别开风气、一新天下人耳目的是苏轼。他几乎无所不写:游仙、咏史、宴赏、登临、悼亡、送别等均有写及。他是最早把武备和统一的题材带到词里的作家之一,如《江城子》"持节云中,何日遣冯唐?"一般认为苏轼是自比防御匈奴的云中太守魏尚,一说他是自比持节去赦免云中太守的冯唐,新说比较便于翻译。他的词也有比较深刻反映农村生活的,如《浣溪沙》中的"牛衣古柳卖黄瓜"(一作"半依古柳")。

除了扩大题材之外,苏轼的主要贡献是豪放词派的创立,名作有《念奴娇》《水调歌头》中秋词等。"中秋词自东坡《水调歌头》一出,余词尽废。"[1]开头"明月几时有?把酒问青天"两句,夏承焘认为是从李白《把酒问月》诗中"青天有月来

---

[1] 见胡仔《苕溪渔隐丛话》。

几时？我今停杯一问之"两句脱化而来。①靳极苍的解说却是："这样完美的明月能完美多长时间呢？"又说："讲作问月是什么年代有的，对抒发作者的情感有什么关系呢？"②我在《苏东坡诗词新译》中采用了夏说，这里的译文改从靳说。这首词"胸怀开朗，不消极悲观，在写离别之情的词里，可算是独创一格的"③。

苏轼豪放词的代表作是《念奴娇·赤壁怀古》，胡云翼说：这首词"主要是反映他对英雄事业的向往和不能施展抱负的精神苦闷。前段写赤壁雄奇的景色，从景色衬托出三国时火烧赤壁的英雄人物；后段着重写周瑜辉煌的战功，用来反衬自己在事业上没有什么成就"。"羽扇纶巾"，一说指周瑜，一说指诸葛亮。最近发表了郭沫若的遗作《读诗札记四则》④，郭沫若在《大江东去》中说："东坡幻想的词中世界（'故国神游'），在赤壁之战时有小乔参加。出场人物为周瑜、小乔、诸葛亮，连东坡自己也加进去了，因为他在'神游'。"又说："'多情'即指小乔。赤壁之战的当时，周瑜年二十四岁，诸葛亮年二十七岁。小乔不用说更加年轻。《赤壁怀古》作于宋神宗元丰五年壬戌（1082），东坡年四十七岁。由于'神游'而加入一群古人之中，以他为最年老，故说小乔笑他有了白头发。"这幅画面画得很入神。郭沫若说的周瑜年岁有误，历史上的诸葛亮在赤壁之战前作为刘备的特使，到东吴搬了救兵就回去了，东坡恐怕不会以为他参加了赤壁之战。但是"多情"即指小乔之说很美，所

---

① 见夏承焘《唐宋词欣赏》。
② 见靳极苍《唐宋词百首详解》。
③ 见胡云翼《唐宋词一百首》。
④ 见1982年11月16日《光明日报》。

以这里的译文改用了郭说。

周笃文说:"东坡的词风是不拘一格的。豪放之外,还有多种色调。有的韶秀,有的秾丽,有的温婉,有的蕴藉,真如万花生春,令人目不暇接。就拿《水龙吟·次韵章质夫杨花词》来说,以健笔写柔情,能于豪宕之中寓缠绵之致,是很出色的……词中的杨花,实际上是抛家傍路、任人蹂躏的女性的化身,作者以深厚的同情之笔来描写,这种拟人的写法是很成功的。东坡的小令也很有特色。"像这里选译的《定风波》和《蝶恋花》,"前者简淡而后者秾丽,却又有一个共同点,即反映出作者随遇而安的坦荡胸怀来"。①

黄庭坚是苏门四学士之一,他的诗为江西派的宗主,词却早年近柳,多写艳情,晚年近苏,深于感慨。这里选译的一首惜春词《清平乐》,可以和王观的惜春词《卜算子》相比较。

秦观也是苏门四学士之一。以词而论,他的成就更为突出,是婉约派一个代表人物。这里选译了他的《鹊桥仙》和《踏莎行》。"两情若是久长时,又岂在朝朝暮暮!"是歌颂真挚爱情的名句。"郴江幸自绕郴山,为谁流下潇湘去!"是"东坡绝爱"的名句。靳极苍解释说:"这是暗喻的方法:秦观哪,你自己在自己家乡多好呀,为何你偏偏要离了家乡出外谋求什么呢!这是深自责悔的意思。或解为'不耐山城寂寞'(见胡云翼《宋词选》),太不了解当时作者的心情了。"②这里的译文采用了靳说。

贺铸是苏门词友之一。我选译的《捣练子》写洗衣女怀念远征的亲人,这种主题的作品在唐诗中很多,宋词里却很

---

① 见周笃文《宋词》。
② 见靳极苍《唐宋词百首详解》。

少见。《鹧鸪天》是一首追悼亡妻的词，词里没有什么奇情幻想，只是写眼前的景象，谈日常的琐事和朴素的感触，却表现出深厚的感情，可以和苏轼的悼亡词《江城子》相比。这里还选了一首李之仪的《卜算子》。毛晋《姑溪词跋》说他"小令更长于淡语、景语、情语"。

周邦彦精通音乐，他的词格律很严密，被称为婉约派的集大成者和格律派的创始人。这里选译了他的《苏幕遮》和《蝶恋花》。《苏幕遮》是咏荷花的名作，词人从汴京的荷花想起了故乡的荷花，想得入神，仿佛做梦似的划着船进入荷花丛里去了。王国维在《人间词话》中说："此真能得荷之神理者。"

北宋末期登上词坛的李清照，是我国文学史上杰出的女词人。美国加州州立大学许芥昱教授在美国现代语言学会第77期学报上发表关于李清照词的论文，说她的词有五个特点：第一，口语入词，如这里选译的《凤凰台上忆吹箫》。第二，形象生动，如《永遇乐》中的"落日镕金，暮云合璧"。第三，善用叠字，如《声声慢》中的"寻寻觅觅"。第四，音乐性强，如《声声慢》。第五，借景写情，如在《如梦令》中，借海棠"绿肥红瘦"之景，写词人惜春而不伤春之情，用了孟浩然"夜来风雨声，花落知多少"的诗意，却又更加含蓄，更加曲折。

自然，李清照词的五个特点，几乎在每首词中都有所体现。如这里选译的《醉花阴》，就既形象生动，又音乐性强，还借重阳黄花之景，写出了词人相思之情。开头的"薄雾浓云"，夏承焘认为是比喻香炉出来的香烟，我的译文采用了这种解说。又如《一剪梅》，也是五个特点都具备的名作。"独上兰舟"有两种解说：一说指赵明诚，一说指李清照。还是译作词人好和下文相关联。关于最著名的《声声慢》，夏承焘说：末了几句"二十多个字里,舌音、齿音交相垂迭,是有意以这种声调来表达她心中的忧郁和怅惘。这些句子不但读起来明白如话,听起来也有明显的音乐美,充分体现出这种配乐文学的特色"。又说:"这首词借双声叠韵字来增强表达感情的效果,是从前词家不大运用的艺术手法。"① 我的译文也尽可能用短音押韵,如译文第一行最后一字和原文第一句的"觅"字,译文第四行最后一字和原文第三句的"戚"字,不但元音相近,连前面的辅音也相同,目的是要尽可能地传达原词的特点。

北宋末期的抗金名将岳飞写了一些爱国主义的词篇,最著名的是《满江红》"怒发冲冠"。有人怀疑它可能是赝品,靳极苍在《唐宋词百首详解》中做了解答,他认为"八千里路云和月"一句的意思是:"八千里转战收复的土地,像浮云像水月一样,成了空的了。""贺兰山缺"是"象征着、代表着敌人的屯驻所,是以专有名词作普通名词用的"。最后他说:"我们可以极高兴地宣告,《满江红·怒发冲冠》是我国最伟大的爱国将领、爱国词人岳飞的抒怀述志的伟大诗篇。"我的译文采用了靳说。岳飞另写了一首《满江红·登黄鹤楼有感》,他写这首词的墨迹现在还可以看得到。唐圭璋等编的《唐宋词选注》中说:"此墨迹见近人徐用仪所编《五千年来中华民族爱国魂》卷端。"

1126年靖康事变之后,在南渡的前期,有一些词人如朱敦儒、陈与义等,风格本来接近周邦彦,靖康事变的巨大冲击使他们起了思想变化。如陈与义的《临江仙》作于乱后,全词浸透了悲凉的情绪。又如朱敦儒的《相见欢》也是南渡后的作品,周笃文认为这首词"慷慨悲凉,回肠荡气,声可

---

① 见夏承焘《唐宋词欣赏》。

裂竹，是爱国词中难得的精品"。

南宋前期的爱国词人还有张元干和张孝祥。张元干因反对秦桧的投降路线，弃官归里。胡铨曾上书朝廷请斩秦桧，结果遭到迫害，张元干写了有名的《贺新郎》为他送行，词中批判的锋芒直接指向了皇帝，忠愤满纸。张孝祥在1154年状元及第，官至建康留守，后被谗言中伤落职，路过洞庭湖时写了一首《念奴娇》。"孤光自照，肝胆皆冰雪"正是他人格的写照。"尽挹西江"三句，以北斗为杯，以江水为酒，以自然为体，清旷放达，真可与东坡比肩。他和张元干的爱国词作，对辛弃疾有积极的影响，可以说是辛词的前驱。

陆游是著名的爱国诗人，词只是他的一种"余事"，但他那忧国伤时的怀抱，也同样深沉地从词里喷涌出来。如《诉衷情》可以说是忠愤之作；《卜算子·咏梅》中的梅花，则是他人格的化身，不论风吹雨打，碾压成泥，也不改其芳洁。他被迫和爱妻唐婉离异，1155年春天，二人相遇于沈园，唐婉以黄滕酒殷勤款待，陆游就在沈园墙上写下了著名的《钗头凤》。唐婉和词如下：

世情薄，人情恶，雨送黄昏花易落。
晓风干，泪痕残，欲笺心事，独语斜阑。
难，难，难！
人成各，今非昨，病魂常似秋千索。
角声寒，夜阑珊，怕人寻问，咽泪装欢。
瞒，瞒，瞒！

这是现实生活中的宝、黛悲剧，却比宝、黛早了五六百年。南宋词坛最杰出的豪放派代表是辛弃疾，他22岁时参加了耿京的抗金义军。但是叛徒张安国杀害了耿京,投降了金人,辛弃疾就率领五十人马,直冲金兵营盘,活捉了张安国,南渡长江,把他押到临安正法。这事在《鹧鸪天》"壮岁旌旗"中有追忆描写。他在义军中的生活,《破阵子》一词中也有记述。但是南渡之后,他的抗金建议没有被朝廷采纳。眼见岁月蹉跎,不能有所作为,他非常痛苦,就写下了著名的《水龙吟·登建康赏心亭》。他还用婉转曲折的方式表达他的爱国思想,如著名的《摸鱼儿》就用象征手法,借春事阑珊来比喻国势危殆。词中被妒的"蛾眉",就是作者自己的写照,而"玉环、飞燕"却是暗指投降派。不过他的爱国思想并不是完全消极悲观的,如《菩萨蛮·书江西造口壁》中,他虽然说"西北望长安,可怜无数山",接着下片又说"青山遮不住,毕竟东流去"。这就是把自己收复失地的雄心壮志,比作冲破重重青山阻碍的江水。比较一下李煜的名句"恰似一江春水向东流",就可以看出李词消极、辛词积极了。他有时也用婉转曲折的方式,来表达自己的雄心壮志,如《青玉案·元夕》就用象征的手法,以一个不爱繁华、站在冷落地方的美人,来比喻自己不肯随波逐流、趋炎附势的性格。比较一下李清照的元夕词《永遇乐》:"怕见夜间出去。不如向帘儿底下,听人笑语。"虽然李清照也流露出思念故国的感情,但比起辛弃疾就要低沉得多了。辛词即使低沉,也有深长的含义,如《采桑子》中的"欲说还休",套用了李清照《凤凰台上忆吹箫》中的"多少事欲说还休",但李词"欲说"的是离怀别苦,辛词"欲说"的却是抗金大业。

辛弃疾在江西农村闲居先后达20年之久,写下了不少农村词。但他即使身在农村,还是不忘国事,如《清平乐·独宿博山王氏庵》中说"布被秋宵梦觉,眼前万里江山",就是在梦中也不忘收复失地。他也写了一些关于农村生活的小令，如这里选译的《鹧鸪天》《清平乐·村居》《西江月·夜行黄沙道中》等。关于《西江月·夜行黄沙道中》，刘瑞明在《"明月别枝惊鹊"及其他》①一文中说："'别枝'二字，俞平伯先生认为是'另一枝'，朱光潜先生认为是'离别树枝'。……人们大都认为明月惊动了鹊……明月有惊鹊的可能，但此处惊鹊的却是夜行的作者，而非明月。……词的语言从表面上看是写夜行之景，从内容上详析，主旨仍在写夜行情趣。诗人有两惊三喜。鹊惊反使己惊，这是一惊。……骤雨要来了，能赶到客店吗？这是二惊。初惊之后会意过来觉得有趣……是行程中偶得之趣。'稻花香里说丰年……'这是全程之喜。……忽而见到前次住过的茅店，不用愁遇雨了，又是惊而转喜。这两惊三喜既写了丰收在望时夜行，人人共有之喜，也写了诗人此夜此行独有的乐趣。"

辛弃疾的农村词和苏东坡的《浣溪沙》五首有所不同：东坡的农村词是写太守与民同乐，他的"稻花香里说丰年"，却把自己放在和农民同等的地位。他的"以手推松曰去"是用口语入词、散文入词的好例子。夏承焘说："用散文句法入词，用经史典故入词，这都是辛弃疾豪放词风格的特色之一。"

直到66岁，辛弃疾才被起用为镇江知府。当时宰相韩侂胄仓促北伐，辛弃疾建议要做好准备，却又受到降职处分。他就写了著名的《永遇乐·京口北固亭怀古》，词中歌颂孙权、刘裕能够抵抗北方的强敌，谴责刘裕的儿子轻率北伐的失败，自比不受重视的老将廉颇，后来韩侂胄果然战败被诛。这首词中的典故很多，但是多和镇江史实、眼前风光有关。

---

① 见《文学评论》1983年第1期。

他还写了《南乡子·登京口北固亭有怀》，和《永遇乐》一样反映了时代的矛盾冲突，周笃文认为他"超过了其他词人，代表了宋词的最高成就"。

辛词的影响十分深远，和他同时的陈亮、刘过，稍后的刘克庄、刘辰翁、文天祥等，都深受他的影响。这里选译了刘过的《西江月》，却是赞成韩侂胄北伐的词，但词中对韩推崇过高了。陈亮也是辛派词人，他与辛弃疾交谊很深。这里选译了他的《水调歌头·送章德茂大卿使虏》。词中对南宋派出章德茂到金朝去祝贺新年，深感不满。他借送行的机会写下这首词，表现了强烈的民族自尊心和对女真贵族的深仇大恨，并且满怀信心，认为消灭敌人、恢复中原的时机必然会到来。

高涨的爱国思想潮流，在词坛上大约维持了80余年，就逐渐为姜夔等人的风雅词派所代替。姜词继承了周邦彦格律精严的传统，词句精练，风格不俗，这里选译了他早期的代表作《扬州慢》。词中以当日的盛况衬托眼前的荒芜，构思巧妙，对比强烈，色彩鲜明，是一首感念世乱的佳作。但他的某些咏物作品，一味堆砌典故，内容空洞，流弊所及，渐开了雕饰藻绘的词匠之风，影响却不太好。

姜夔之后，词坛的领袖是吴文英，他是南宋后期格律派代表人物之一。他写词注重锤炼词句，但是忽视内容思想。这里选译的《八声甘州》是吴词中内容比较充实的一首，淡淡地透露了词人对国事的隐忧。他和姜夔一样偏重形式技巧，使词坛上形式主义的潮流有进一步发展。

姜、吴词风笼罩词坛的时候，也有词人坚持苏、辛一派的道路，如刘克庄。这里选译了他的《玉楼春·戏林推》，这首词寓庄于谐，规劝友人不要日夜花天酒地，狂嫖滥赌，忘了光复神州的大业。

南宋末年的民族英雄文天祥也写了一些大义凛然的词篇，这里选译了他被押北上、路过金陵时写给友人邓剡的《念奴娇》，一说这词是邓剡作的。另外还选译了他的《沁园春·题潮阳张许二公庙》，词中充满了昂扬的爱国精神。

　　南宋亡后，元兵进入临安（今杭州），继续抵抗的朝臣逃往海上。这里选译了一首南宋遗民刘辰翁的《柳梢青》，词中写了临安陷落后一个元宵灯节的景象，可和辛词《青玉案》对比。此外，选译了一首张炎的《清平乐》，词中曲折反映了作者国破家亡之痛，流浪无依之苦，可和张先的《玉楼春》对比。

　　这本词集共选唐宋词100首，主要选自胡云翼所编《唐宋词一百首》。这篇前言主要依据周笃文《宋词》一书，兼采各家之说写成。译文全都押韵，希望能使读者认识这个"毋庸置疑的充满魅力、抒情性强和意境深邃的世界"，闻到"这个世界里洋溢着书面上看到的花朵的香气"，欣赏这"三千多年悠久文化与文明的结晶"。

许渊冲译唐宋词一百首

鹊踏枝

[唐] 无名氏

叵耐①灵鹊②多谩语③,
送喜何曾有凭据。
几度飞来活捉取,
锁上金笼④休共语⑤。
比拟⑥好心来送喜,
谁知锁我在金笼里。
欲他征夫⑦早归来,
腾身⑧却放我向青云里。

① 叵（pǒ）耐：不可忍耐，可恨。
② 灵鹊：相传是能够传报喜讯的鹊，又称喜鹊。
③ 谩语：欺骗的语言，这里指谎话。
④ 金笼：坚固而又精美的鸟笼。
⑤ 休共语：不要和他说话。
⑥ 比拟：打算，准备。
⑦ 征夫：出远门的人。这里是指关锁灵鹊的人的丈夫。
⑧ 腾身：跃身而起。

Tune: The Magpie on a Branch

Anonymous

How can I bear to hear the chattering magpie
Announce the happy news on which I can't rely?
So thus I catch it alive when it flies to me again
And shut it in a cage where lonely 'twill remain.
—With good intent I brought her a happy message.
Who would expect she'd shut me in a golden cage?
I wish her husband would come back soon so that I
Might be set free and take my flight to the blue sky.

This is a popular song written by an unknown poet of the Tang Dynasty (618—907) and unearthed in one of the chapels in the Thousand Buddha Caves at Dunhuang, Gansu, in 1900. Unlike a literary lyric in which everything is seen through the eye of the persona, this song presents two distinct points of view by using a dialogue between a woman who waits in vain for the return of her husband, and a magpie who is supposed to announce the expected arrival.

摊破浣溪沙①

[唐] 无名氏

五里滩头风欲平,
张帆举棹②觉船轻。
柔橹不施③停却棹——
是船行。
满眼风波多闪灼④,
看山恰似走来迎。
子细⑤看山山不动——
是船行。

① 摊破浣溪沙:词牌名。
② 张帆举棹:张起帆篷,打起船桨。棹,船桨。
③ 柔橹不施:橹桨也可以不用摇了。柔橹,一种用来拨水推动船前进的器具。施,使用。
④ 闪灼:水面上波光闪动的样子。
⑤ 子细:通"仔细"。

Tune: Broken Form of Sand of Silk-washing Stream

Anonymous

After passing the five li beach, the breeze stops blowing,
With sails unfurled, the boat seems light when we are rowing.
We use no scull and take our oars from water flowing,
But still the boat is going.
The water shimmers in the breeze before the eye;
As if to bid us welcome, the mountain comes nigh,
On a close look, it does not move but towers high:
The boat is going by.

This is another popular song unearthed at Dunhuang. It depicts the life and joy of a boatman.

菩萨蛮

[唐] 李 白

平林漠漠烟如织,
寒山一带伤心碧。
暝色①入高楼,
有人楼上愁。
玉阶空伫立②,
宿鸟归飞急。
何处是归程?
长亭③更短亭。

① 暝色:幽暗、昏暗的天色,这里指暮色。
② 伫立:长久地站立。
③ 长亭:行人休息或者饯别之处。所谓"十里一长亭,五里一短亭"。

Tune: Buddhist Dancers

Li Bai

O'er far-flung wooded plain wreaths of smoke weave a screen,

Cold mountains stretch into a belt of sorrowful green.

The dusk invades the tower high

Where someone sighs a longing sigh.

On marble steps she waits in vain

But to see birds fly back amain.

Where should she gaze to find her dear?

She sees but stations far and near.

As early as the Northern Song Dynasty (960—1127), this poem and the following were considered to be the two earliest literary lyrics written by Li Bai (701—762). This poem describes the sorrow of a young woman who mounts a high tower at dusk, looks far into the wooded plain and the belt-like mountains, but fails to find her husband on his way home.

忆秦娥

[唐] 李 白

箫声咽①,

秦娥②梦断秦楼月。

秦楼月,

年年柳色,

灞陵③伤别。

乐游原④上清秋节,

咸阳⑤古道音尘绝。

音尘绝⑥,

西风残照,

汉家陵阙⑦。

---

① 箫声咽:据《列仙传》载:"萧史者,秦穆公时人也。善吹箫,能致孔雀、白鹤于庭。穆公有女字弄玉,好之。公遂妻焉。日教弄玉作凤鸣。居数年,吹似凤声,凤凰来止其屋。公为作凤台。夫妇止其上,不下数年,一旦皆随凤凰飞去。"咽,声音受阻而低沉。
② 秦娥:泛指秦地美貌女子。
③ 灞陵:故址在今陕西省西安市东,因有汉文帝墓而名。附近有灞桥,为唐人送客的折柳告别之处。
④ 乐游原:唐代的游览胜地,故址在今陕西西安市南。
⑤ 咸阳:今陕西省咸阳市。汉唐时期,从长安西去,咸阳为必经之地。
⑥ 音尘绝:音信断绝。
⑦ 汉家陵阙:汉朝皇帝的陵墓都建在长安四周。阙,陵墓前的楼观。

Tune: Dream of a Maid of Honour

Li Bai

The flute plays a sobbing tune,

She wakes from dreams when o'er her bower wanes the moon.

When o'er her bower wanes the moon,

Year after year green willows grieve

As from the Bridge the people leave.

All's merry on Clear Autumn Day,

But she receives no word from ancient northwest way.

And now o'er ancient northwest way

The sun declines, the west wind falls

O'er royal tombs and palace walls.

This lyric depicts the solitude of a young woman who wakes from a dream of her husband on the eve of Clear Autumn Day or Mountain-climbing Day, that is, the 9th day of the 9th lunar month. It recalls his parting with her at the Bridge east of the capital. She then goes to the Merry-making Plain where she waits until sunset without seeing a messenger coming from her husband, another commentator says that the people taking leave were those who were going to the war against the rebels in 755, so this lyric predicted the decline and fall of the Tang Empire.

长相思

[唐]白居易

汴水①流,
泗水②流,
流到瓜洲古渡③头。
吴山④点点愁。
思悠悠,
恨悠悠,
恨到归时方始休。
月明人倚楼。

① 汴(biàn)水:又名汴渠,自荥阳与黄河分流,向东南汇入淮河。
② 泗(sì)水:河流的名称,发源于山东省济宁市,流经曲阜、徐州等地,至洪泽湖附近入淮河。
③ 瓜洲古渡:在江苏省扬州市南长江北岸。瓜洲本为江中沙洲,沙渐长,状如瓜字,故名。
④ 吴山:在浙江省杭州市,春秋时为吴国南界,故名。

Tune: Everlasting Longing

Bai Juyi

See the Bian River flow

And the Si River flow!

By Ancient Ferry, mingling waves, they go,

The Southern hills reflect my woe.

My thought stretches endlessly,

My grief wretches endlessly,

So thus until my husband comes to me,

Alone on moon-lit balcony.

Bai Juyi (772—846) was a popular realistic poet who served as official in the south of the Yangzi River. This lyric depicts the longing of a young woman for the return of her husband. Leaning on the railings of a balcony on a moon-lit night, she sees the two rivers meet at the ancient ferry where people used to bid farewell, but where she cannot find her husband home-coming, so she feels the hills there saddened by her grief.

渔歌子

[唐]张志和

西塞山①前白鹭飞。
桃花流水鳜鱼②肥。
青箬笠③,
绿蓑衣,
斜风细雨不须归。

① 西塞山:道士矶,位于今湖北省大冶县长江边。
② 鳜鱼:俗称"花鱼""桂鱼",是一种味道鲜美的鱼。
③ 箬笠:用一种箬竹的叶子编制成的斗笠,用来遮雨或者遮阳光。

Tune: A Fisherman's Song

Zhang Zhihe

In front of western hills white egrets fly up and down,

In peach-mirrored stream mandarin fish are full grown.

In my blue bamboo hat

And green straw cloak, I'd fain

Go fishing careless of slanting wind and fine rain.

Zhang Zhihe (730—782) served in the court as a petty official and then retired to the riverside and lived in seclusion. This poem describing the happiness of a fisherman was wide spread and soon reached Japan. Even the Japanese Emperor (reigned 804—823) wrote five lyrics following the rhyme of his poem.

竹枝词

[唐] 刘禹锡

山桃红花满上头,
蜀江春水拍山流。
花红易衰似郎意,
水流无限似侬①愁。

① 侬:指我,古代吴人的自称。

Tune: Bamboo Branch Song

Liu Yuxi

The mountain's red with peach blossoms above;
The shore is washed by spring water below.
Red blossoms will fade as my gallant's love;
The river as my sorrow will e'er flow.

Liu Yuxi (772—842) was well known for his popular songs which depict the life and love of the common people. This song displays a happy combination of natural scenery and inner feeling of the persona.

浪淘沙

[唐] 刘禹锡

日照澄洲①江雾开,
淘金女伴满江隈②。
美人首饰侯王印。
尽是沙中浪底来。

① 澄洲:清澈的江水环绕着的小沙滩。
② 江隈(wēi):江水弯曲之处。

Tune: Ripples Sifting Sand

Liu Yuxi

The sun dispels the mist and shines on river-strand,
The crook is crowd'd with women washing gold from sand.
The seals of kings and lords, tinsels of ladies fair
Are taken from the sand and by these poor women's care.

In this poem the reader will find a striking contrast between the women washing gold-bearing gravel in the river and the fair ladies wearing gold tinsels in the palace.

梦江南

[唐]温庭筠

梳洗罢,
独①倚望江楼②。
过尽千帆③皆④不是,
斜晖⑤脉脉⑥水悠悠。
肠断白蘋洲。

① 独:独自。
② 望江楼:楼名,因为临江而得名。
③ 千帆:上千只帆船。帆,船上使用风力的布篷,一般作为船的代名词。
④ 皆:都。
⑤ 斜晖:日落前的日光。晖,阳光。
⑥ 脉脉:脉脉含情达意的样子,这里是运用拟人的手法。

Tune: Dreaming of the South

Wen Tingyun

After dressing my hair,

I alone climb the stair.

On the railings I lean,

To view the river scene.

Many sails pass me by,

But not the one for which wait I.

The slanting sun sheds a sympathetic ray,

The carefree river carries it away.

My heart breaks at the sight

Of the islet with duckweed white.

Wen Tingyun (813—870) was traditionally regarded as the first major lyricist. His lyrics are richly embellished and full of implicit meaning, but this poem simply narrates in the folk-song manner the sorrow of a young woman who, gazing on the river and the islet where people used to bid farewell, is waiting all day long for the return of her husband.

河传

[唐]温庭筠

湖上,
闲望。
雨萧萧,
烟浦花桥路遥。
谢娘翠蛾①愁不销,
终朝②。
梦魂迷晚潮。
荡子天涯归棹③远。
春已晚,
莺语空肠断。
若耶溪④,
溪水西。
柳堤,
不闻郎马嘶。

① 翠蛾:青绿色的眼眉。
② 终朝:一整天。
③ 棹:船桨。
④ 若耶溪:小溪的名字,传说西施曾在这里浣沙,位于今浙江省绍兴市若耶山下。

Tune: From the River

Wen Tingyun

Unoccupied

By the lakeside,

She gazes on far-flung pathways,

Flowery bridges and beach in rainy haze.

It's a sad sight the songstress fair

Knitting her soft brows cannot bear

All the day long.

How can she forget the evening tidal song?

Where is his boat which has to roam

Far, far from her and far from home?

It is late spring,

And her heart will break to hear orioles sing.

Taking a look,

West of the brook,

At the long willowy pathway,

She cannot hear the horse of the roamer neigh.

This lyric depicts the sorrow of a fair songstress who, gazing in the rain on the pathway where her beloved parted from her, and remembering the evenings they used to spend together, is waiting in vain for his return.

忆江南

[唐] 皇甫松

兰烬①落,
屏上暗红蕉②。
闲梦江南梅熟日,
夜船吹笛雨萧萧③,
人语驿④边桥。

---

① 兰烬:因为烛光似兰,所以这里代指蜡烛。烬,物体燃烧后剩下的部分。
② 暗红蕉:这里的意思是夜深人静,蜡烛燃尽,画屏上的美人图画变得模糊不清。
③ 萧萧:通"潇潇",形容雨声。
④ 驿:驿亭,古时公差或者行人暂歇之处。

Tune: The South Recalled

Huangfu Song

Candle-wick burned,

Red cannas painted on the screen dark turned.

I dreamed of mume-fruit rip'ring on the Southern shore,

Of flute-songs played adrift one rainy night of yore,

Of whispers lost

In running stream below the bridge beside the post.

Huangfu Song was one of the precursors of the lyric poets of the "School among Flowers". This lyric describes one of his dreams on a night when the candle-wick was burned out, it reveals his nostalgia for the Southern country.

菩萨蛮

[唐] 韦 庄

人人尽说江南好,
游人只合①江南老。
春水碧于天,
画船听雨眠。
垆边②人似月,
皓腕③凝霜雪。
未老莫还乡,
还乡须④断肠。

① 只合:只应,只当。
② 垆边:暗用汉代卓文君当垆卖酒的典故。垆,酒店安放酒坛的土台子。
③ 皓腕:洁白的手臂。
④ 须:应该。

Tune: Buddhist Dancers

Wei Zhuang

All men will say the Southern land is fair,
A wanderer is willing to spend his whole life there,
He'd like to see spring water bluer than the sky
And, listening to rain, in painted ship to lie.
The wine-shop waitress looks like the moon bright,
Like snow or frost congealed her arms are white.
Till he grows old, from South lands he won't part,
To leave this land for home would break his heart.

Wei Zhuang (836—910) was considered one of the leaders of the "School among Flowers". In contrast to the ornate rhetoric of other lyric poets of this School, his diction is simple and direct and explicit. In this lyric is revealed a Northerner's love for the beautiful Southern land.

南乡子

[唐] 李　珣

乘彩舫①,
过莲塘②,
棹歌③惊起睡鸳鸯。
游女带花偎伴笑④,
争窈窕⑤,
竞折团荷⑥遮晚照。

① 彩舫：华美的小船。
② 莲塘：种植荷花的水塘。
③ 棹歌：划船的时候唱的歌。
④ 偎伴笑：和伙伴紧紧靠在一起笑。
⑤ 窈窕：体态优美、灵活和轻巧。
⑥ 团荷：圆形的荷叶。

Tune: Song of a Southern Country

Li Xun

A skiff goes along

A lotus pond,

Sleeping lovebirds start at oarswomen's song.

Perfumed maidens leaning on each other make fun,

Vying to be the fairest one,

They take round lotus leaves to shun

The setting sun.

Li Xun was a lyric poet of the "School among Flowers". His lyrics are full of local color.

酒泉子

[唐] 孙光宪

空碛①无边,

万里阳关道路②。

马萧萧③,

人去去,

陇④云愁。

香貂旧制戎衣窄,

胡霜千里白。

绮罗心,

魂梦隔,

上高楼。

---

① 空碛(qì):空旷的大沙漠。
② 阳关道路:原指阳关通往西北地区的大道,这里泛指通往边塞的道路。
③ 萧萧:马鸣声。
④ 陇:陇山,古代防御吐蕃侵扰的军事要地。

Tune: Fountain of Wine

Sun Guangxian

The boundless desert looked desolate,

Long, long the road to Southern Gate.

Your horse was heard to neigh,

You were seen on your way,

E'en border clouds felt sad.

The sable coat in which you're clad

May be outworn, your uniform too tight,

The thousand-li Northwest frontier with frost is white.

In silk I'm dressed,

But my heart cannot fly

In dreams to the Northwest,

So I mount the tower high.

Sun Guangxian (900—968) was a lyric poet of the "School among Flowers". This lyric depicts a young woman recalling her husband parting from her for the Southern Gate in the northwest border, thinking of him when frost fails in the desert, and feeling grieved that she could not go to see him even in her dreams.

谒金门

[南唐] 冯延巳

风乍①起,
吹绉一池春水。
闲引②鸳鸯芳径里,
手挼③红杏蕊。
斗鸭④阑干独倚,
碧玉搔头⑤斜坠。
终日望君君不至,
举头闻鹊喜。

① 乍:忽然。
② 闲引:无聊地逗引着玩。
③ 挼(ruó):揉搓。
④ 斗鸭:以鸭相斗为欢乐。古代也有斗鸡之说,都是官僚显贵无聊取乐的玩法。
⑤ 碧玉搔头:碧玉簪。

Tune: Paying Homage at the Golden Gate

Feng Yansi

The breeze begins to blow

And it ruffles a pool of spring water below.

Crushing pink apricot petals in hand, I play

With a pair of lovebirds on the fragrant pathway.

Seeing ducks fight, alone on the railings I lean,

Slanting upon my head a hairpin of jade green.

Waiting for you the whole day long wears out my eyes,

Raising my head, I'm glad to hear magpies.

Feng Yansi (903—960) was prime minister in the court of the second ruler of the Late Tang Dynasty (937—975). His lyrics show the subtle refinement of a courtier. In this well-known lyric he paints a leisure-class lady who has nothing to do all day long, whose mind is like a pool ruffled by a sudden breeze while waiting for her husband, and who is glad to hear the magpies chatter, which is supposed to announce the expected arrival.

破阵子

[南唐] 李 煜

四十年来家国,
三千里地山河。
凤阁龙楼连霄汉,
玉树琼枝作烟萝。
几曾识干戈?
一旦归为臣虏,
沈腰①潘鬓②消磨。
最是仓皇辞庙③日,
教坊④犹奏别离歌,
垂泪对宫娥。

① 沈腰:细腰,这里指腰围减小。
② 潘鬓:指中年鬓发早白。
③ 庙:古代帝王、诸侯或者大夫祭祀祖宗的场所,宗庙。
④ 教坊:古代官署名称,主管宫乐。

Tune: Dance of the Cavalry

Li Yu

A reign of forty years

O'er a land of three thousand li,

My royal palaces touching the celestial spheres,

My shady forest looking like a hazy sea.

What did I know of shields and spears?

A captive now, I'm worn away,

Thinner I grow, my hair turns gray.

O how could I forget the hurried parting day

When by the band the farewell songs were played

And I shed tears before my palace maid!

Li Yu (937—978) was the last ruler of the Later Tang Dynasty. In 975, his capital fell and he himself was taken captive. In his captivity he wrote many of his best lyrics which represent the highest achievement of the lyric poets of that period. In this lyric we find a sharp contrast between the past in the first stanza and the present in the second.

相见欢

[南唐] 李 煜

无言独上西楼,
月如钩。
寂寞梧桐深院锁清秋[①]。
剪不断,
理还乱,
是离愁[②]。
别是一般滋味[③]在心头。

---

① 锁清秋:深深地被凄清的秋色所笼罩。
② 离愁:指离开国家的忧愁。
③ 别是一般滋味:一作"别是一番滋味",这里是另有一种滋味的意思。

Tune: Joy at Meeting

Li Yu

Silent, I climb the Western Tower alone

And see the hook-like moon.

Parasol-trees lonesome and drear

Lock in the courtyard autumn clear.

Cut, it won't sever;

Be ruled, 'twill never.

What sorrow'tis to part!

It's an unspeakable taste in the heart.

This is one of the best lyrics describing the sorrow of separation. We can find that after an implicit description of his loneliness in the first stanza, the poet utters three short lines mirroring the intensity of his sorrow and then the final line revealing the relaxation of his feeling.

乌夜啼[①]

[南唐] 李 煜

林花谢[②]了春红,

太匆匆。

无奈朝来寒雨晚来风。

胭脂泪[③],

留人醉。

几时重[④]?

自是人生长恨水长东。

① 乌夜啼:又名"相见欢""秋夜月""上西楼"。词牌名。
② 谢:凋谢。
③ 胭脂泪:指女子的眼泪。女子脸上搽有胭脂,泪水流经脸颊时沾上胭脂的红色。
④ 几时重:何时再度相会。

Tune: Crows Crying at Night

Li Yu

Spring's rosy color fades from forest flowers
Too soon, too soon.
How can they bear cold morning showers
And winds at noon!
Your rouged tears like crimson rain
Intoxicate my heart.
When shall we meet again?
As water eastward flows, so shall we part.

The image of crimson flowers filling in the cold morning rain is compared to the rouged tears of a beautiful woman the poet is going to leave. Through this image he conveys the idea that even the external world shares his personal sorrow.

浪淘沙①

[南唐] 李 煜

帘外雨潺潺②,
春意阑珊③。
罗衾④不耐⑤五更寒。
梦里不知身是客,
一晌⑥贪欢⑦。

独自莫凭阑,
无限江山。
别时容易见时难。
流水落花春去也,
天上人间!

① 此词原为唐教坊曲,又名"浪淘沙令""卖花声"等。
② 潺潺:形容雨声。
③ 阑珊:不兴旺、衰败的样子。
④ 罗衾:绸缎被子。
⑤ 不耐:受不了。
⑥ 一晌:一会儿、片刻。
⑦ 贪欢:指贪恋梦境中的快乐。

Tune: Ripples Sifting Sand

Li Yu

The curtain cannot keep out the patter of rain,

Springtime is on the wane.

In the deep of the night my quilt is not cold-proof.

Forgetting I am under hospitable roof,

Still in my dream I seek for pleasures vain.

Don't lean alone on the railings and

Yearn for the boundless land!

To bid farewell is easier than to meet again.

With flowers fallen on the waves spring's gone amain,

So is the paradise of men.

This is one of the best lyrics written by Li Yu after he was taken as a captive north to the Song capital. Fallen flowers, rolling waves, departing spring, all reminded him of his lost country.

虞美人 [1]

[南唐] 李 煜

春花秋月何时了[2],
往事知多少。
小楼昨夜又东风,
故国不堪回首月明中。

雕栏玉砌[3]应犹在,
只是朱颜改。
问君能有几多愁?
恰似一江春水向东流。

---

[1] 唐教坊曲,又名"一江春水""玉壶水""巫山十二峰"等。双调,五十六字,上下片各四句,皆为两仄转两平韵。
[2] 了:了结,完结。
[3] 雕栏玉砌:雕有图案的栏杆和玉石铺就的台阶。这里泛指宫殿建筑。

Tune: The Beautiful Lady Yu

Li Yu

When will there be no more an autumn moon and spring time flowers
For me who had so many memorable hours?
My attic which last night in the east wind did stand
Reminds me cruelly of the lost moonlit land.

Carved balustrades and marble steps must still be there,
But rosy faces cannot be as fair.
If you would ask me how my sorrow has increased,
Just see the over-brimming river flowing east!

This is supposed to be the last lyric written by Li Yu before his death. As John Mill says, "all poetry is of the nature of soliloquy." "The peculiarity of poetry appears to us to lie in the poet's utter unconsciousness of a listener." Unfortunately, the emperor of the Song Dynasty "overheard" this poem and ordered the poet to take poison. So it may well be said that this lyric epitomizes Nietzeche's concept that all literature must be written in blood.

长相思

[宋] 林　逋

吴山①青,
越山②青,
两岸青山相送迎。
谁知离别情?

君泪盈,
妾泪盈,
罗带同心结未成。
江头潮已平。

① 吴山:泛指钱塘江北岸的群山,古属吴国。
② 越山:泛指钱塘江南岸的群山,古属越国。

Tune: Everlasting Longing

Lin Bu

The northern hills so green,
The southern hills so green,
They greet your ship which sails the river between.
My grief at parting is so keen.

Tears streaming from your eyes,
Tears streaming from my eyes,
In vain we tried to join by marriage ties.
I see the silent river rise.

Lin Bu (967—1028) was a lakeside poet well-known for his verse on mume blossoms. This lyric depicts the sorrow of a young woman who saw her betrothed leave her in a ship when the river rose.

酒泉子

[宋]潘　阆

长①忆观潮,
满郭②人争江上望。
来疑沧海尽成空,
万面鼓声中。

弄潮儿③向涛头立,
手把红旗旗不湿。
别来几向梦中看,
梦觉尚心寒。

① 长：通假字，通"常"，常常、经常。
② 郭：外城，这里指外城以内的范围。
③ 弄潮儿：指朝夕与潮水周旋的水手或在潮中戏水的少年人。

Tune: Fountain of Wine

Pan Lang

I still remember watching tidal bore,
The city poured out people on the shore.
It seemed the sea had emptied all its water here,
And thousands of drums were beating far and near.

At the crest of huge billows the swimmers did stand,
Yet dry remained red flags they held in hand.
Come back, I saw in dreams the tide o'erflow the river;
Awake, I feel my heart with cold still shiver.

This poem presents a rich-colored picture of the tidal bore on the Qiantang River.

昼夜乐

[宋] 柳　永

洞房①记得初相遇,
便只合②长相聚。
何期小会幽欢,
变作别离情绪!
况值阑珊③春色暮,
对满目乱花狂絮。
直恐好风光,
尽随伊归去。

一场寂寞凭谁诉?
算前言总轻负。
早知恁地难拼④,
悔不当初留住。
其奈风流端正外,
更别有系人心处。
一日不思量,
也攒眉千度。

① 洞房:深邃的住室。后多用来指妇女所居的闺阁,现在也指男女新婚之夜所住的地方。
② 只合:只应该。
③ 阑珊:将残、将尽之意。
④ 恁(nèn)地难拼:这样地难过。难拼,指的是难以和离愁相拼。

Tune: Joy of Day and Night

Liu Yong

In nuptial chamber first I saw your face,
I thought we should forever share the place.
The short-lived joy of love, who would believe?
Soon turned into parting grief.
Now late spring has grown old and soon takes leave,
I see a riot of catkins and flowers
Fallen in showers.
I am afraid all the fine scenery
Would go away with thee.

To whom may I tell my solitude?
Thou oft makest light of promise thou hast made.
Had I known the ennui is so hard to elude,
I would then have thee stayed.
What I can't bear to think, thy gallantry apart,
Is something else in thee which captivates my heart.
If one day I don't think of it,
A thousand times my brows would knit.

Liu Yong (987—1053) was the best-known popular lyric poet of the Song Dynasty (960—1279). He adopted and invented a large number of longer "slow tunes" containing more than one hundred characters. This lyric depicts the sorrow of a lonely young bride.

雨霖铃[1]

[宋] 柳 永

寒蝉凄切,
对长亭晚,
骤雨初歇。
都门[2]帐饮无绪,
方留恋处,
兰舟催发。
执手相看泪眼,
竟无语凝噎[3]。
念去去,
千里烟波,
暮霭沉沉楚天阔。

---

① 雨霖铃:词牌名,也作"雨淋铃"。相传唐玄宗入蜀时在雨中听到铃声而想起杨贵妃,故作此曲。
② 都门:国都之门。指北宋的首都汴京(今河南开封)。
③ 凝噎(yē):喉咙哽塞,欲语不出的样子。

Tune: Bells Ringing in the Rain

Liu Yong

Cicadas chill

And drearily shrill,

We stand face to face at an evening hour

Before the pavilion, after a sudden shower.

Can I care for drinking before we part?

At the city gate

Where we're lingering late,

But the boat is waiting for me to depart.

Hand in hand, we gaze at each other's tearful eyes

And burst into sobs with words congealed on our lips.

I'll go my way

Far, far away

On miles and miles of misty waves where sail the ships,

Evening clouds hang low in boundless Southern skies.

This is a famous lyric depicting the sorrow of a pair of lovers bidding farewell before the pavilion at the city gate of the capital.

多情自古伤离别,

更那堪、

冷落清秋节。

今宵酒醒何处?

杨柳岸,

晓风残月。

此去经年①,

应是良辰好景虚设。

便纵有千种风情,

更与何人说。

① 经年:经过一年或若干年。

Parting lovers would grieve as of old.

How could I stand this clear autumn day so cold!

Where shall I be found at day's early break

From wine awake?

Moored by a riverbank planted with willow trees

Beneath the waning moon and in the morning breeze.

I'll be gone for a year.

In vain would good times and fine scenes appear!

However gallant I am on my part,

To whom can I lay bare my heart?

望海潮

[宋] 柳　永

东南形胜[①],
三吴[②]都会,
钱塘自古繁华。
烟柳画桥,
风帘翠幕,
参差十万人家。
云树绕堤沙,
怒涛卷霜雪,
天堑无涯。
市列珠玑[③],
户盈罗绮,
竞豪奢。

---

① 东南形胜：杭州在北宋为两浙路治所，当东南要冲。
② 三吴：即吴兴、吴郡、会稽三郡，在这里泛指今江苏南部和浙江的部分地区。
③ 珠玑：珠是珍珠，玑是一种不圆的珠子。这里泛指珍贵的商品。

Tune: Watching the Tidal Bore

Liu Yong

Scenic splendor to the Southeast of River Blue

And capital of ancient Kingdom Wu,

Qiantang's as flourishing as e'er.

Smoke-like willows form a wind-proof screen,

Adorned with painted bridges and curtains green,

A hundred thousand houses stand here and there.

Upon the banks along the sand,

Cloud-crowned trees stand.

Great waves roll up like snow banks white,

The river extends till it's lost to sight.

Jewels and pearls at the Fair on display,

Satins and silks in splendid array,

People vie in magnificence

And opulence.

This poem dedicated to the governor of Qiantang (present-day Hangzhou and ancient capital of Kingdom Wu to the southeast of the River Blue or the Yangzi River) describes so well the scenic beauties of the city and its West Lake that it was said to have tempted the chieftain of the Jurchen invaders to cross the Yangzi River.

重湖①叠巘②清嘉,

有三秋桂子,

十里荷花。

羌管弄晴,

菱歌泛夜,

嬉嬉钓叟莲娃。

千骑拥高牙③,

乘醉听箫鼓,

吟赏烟霞。

异日图将好景,

归去凤池④夸。

① 重湖:以白堤为界,西湖分为里湖和外湖,所以也叫重湖。
② 巘(yǎn):大山上之小山。
③ 高牙:高矗的军旗,高官出行时的仪仗旗帜。
④ 凤池:原指皇宫禁苑中的池沼,此处指朝廷。

Lake on lake reflects peak on peak which towers,

Late autumn fragrant with osmanthus flowers,

Lotus in full bloom for miles and miles.

Northwestern pipes play with sunlight,

Water chestnut songs are sung by starlight,

Old fishermen and maidens young all beam with smiles.

With flags before and guards behind you come,

Drunken, you may listen to flute and drum,

Chanting praises loud

Of the land 'neath the cloud.

You may picture the fair scene another day

And boast to the Court where you're in proud array.

八声甘州①

[宋]柳 永

对潇潇暮雨洒江天,
一番洗清秋。
渐霜风凄紧,
关河②冷落,
残照当楼。
是处红衰翠减,
苒苒物华休。
唯有长江水,
无语东流。

① 八声甘州:词牌名,原为唐边塞曲。简称"甘州",又名"潇潇雨""宴瑶池"。
② 关河:关塞与河流,此指山河。

Tune: Eight Beats of a Ganzhou Song

Liu Yong

Shower by shower
Besprinkles evening rain the sky
Over the river,
Washing cool the autumn air both far and nigh.
Gradually frost falls and blows the wind so chill
That few people pass by hill or rill,
In fading sunlight drowned is my bower.
Everywhere the red and the green wither away,
There's no more splendor of a sunny day.
Only the waves of River Long
Silently eastward flow along.

This is a famous nostalgic poem in which the natural scenery is tinged with the poet's personal sorrow.

不忍登高临远,

望故乡渺邈,

归思难收。

叹年来踪迹,

何事苦淹留?

想佳人妆楼颙望①,

误几回天际识归舟?

争知我,

倚阑干处,

正恁②凝愁!

---

① 颙(yóng)望:抬头凝望。颙,一作"长"。
② 恁(nèn):如此。

I cannot bear

To climb high and look far, for to gaze where

My native land is lost in mists so thick

Would make my lonely heart homesick.

I sigh to see my rovings year by year.

Why should I linger hopelessly now there, now here?

From her bower my lady fair

Must gaze with longing eye.

How oft has she mistaken homebound sails

On the horizon for those sails of mine?

How could she know that I,

Leaning upon the rails,

With sorrow frozen on my face, for her I pine!

渔家傲

[宋] 范仲淹

塞下①秋来风景异②,

衡阳雁去③无留意。

四面边声④连角⑤起。

千嶂⑥里,

长烟⑦落日孤城闭。

浊酒一杯家万里,

燕然⑧未勒⑨归无计。

羌管悠悠霜满地⑩。

人不寐,

将军白发征夫泪。

① 塞下:边地。
② 风景异:指景物和江南一带的风景不同。
③ 衡阳雁去:湖南省衡阳市南有一座回雁峰,相传雁飞到这里就不再南飞了。
④ 边声:马嘶风号之类的边地荒凉肃杀的声音。
⑤ 角:军中的号角。
⑥ 嶂:像屏障一样并列的山峰。
⑦ 长烟:荒漠里迷茫的烟雾。
⑧ 燕然:山名,指今天内蒙古自治区境内的杭爱山。
⑨ 勒:刻石记功。东汉窦宪追击北匈奴,出塞三千多里,至燕然山刻石记功而还。燕然未勒,指的是边患没有平息,功业没有完成。
⑩ 霜满地:比喻夜深露重。

Tune: Pride of Fishermen

Fan Zhongyan

When autumn comes to the frontier, the scene looks drear,

South-bound wild geese won't stay

E'en for a day.

An uproar rises with horns blowing far and near.

Walled in by peaks, smoke rises straight

At sunset over isolate town with fastened gate.

I hold a cup of wine, yet home is faraway,

The Northwest is not won and I'm obliged to stay.

At the flutes' doleful sound

Over frost-covered ground,

None fall asleep,

The general's hair turns white and soldiers weep.

Fan Zhongyan (989—1052) was vice-premier and commanding general stationed on the northwest frontier from 1040 to 1043. This lyric describes the border scene and depicts the poet's nostalgia.

苏幕遮

[宋]范仲淹

碧云天,

黄叶地。

秋色连波,

波上寒烟翠。

山映斜阳天接水。

芳草无情,

更在斜阳外。

黯乡魂,

追旅思①。

夜夜除非,

好梦留人睡。

明月楼高休独倚。

酒入愁肠,

化作相思泪。

① 追旅思(sì):撇不开羁旅的愁思。追,追随,这里有缠住不放的意思。旅思,旅居在外的愁思。思,心绪,情怀。

Tune: Screened by Southern Curtain

Fan Zhongyan

Emerald clouds above
And yellow leaves below,
O'er autumn-tinted waves, cold, green mists grow.
The sun slants o'er the hills, the waves blend with the sky,
Unfeeling grass grows sweet beyond the mountains high.

A homesick heart
Lost in thoughts deep,
Only sweet dreams each night can retain me in sleep.
Don't lean alone on rails when the bright moon appears!
Wine in sad bowels would turn into nostalgic tears.

This is another lyric of Fan Zhongyan. The poet's feeling merging with the autumn scene became nostalgia just as wine in his sad bowels turned into homesick tears.

玉楼春

乙卯吴兴寒食

[宋] 张 先

龙头舴艋①吴儿竞,
笋柱②秋千游女并③。
芳洲拾翠暮忘归,
秀野踏青来不定。

行云④去后遥山暝,
已放⑤笙歌池院静。
中庭月色正清明,
无数杨花过无影。

① 舴艋:像蚱蜢一样的小船。
② 笋柱:用竹竿做的秋千架。
③ 并:并排。
④ 行云:这里指女子。
⑤ 放:终止。

Tune: Spring in Jade Pavilion

Written on Cold Food Day, 1075

Zhang Xian

The Southerners in dragon-boats contest in speed,
Fair maidens on the bamboo seat swing to and fro.
And picking flowers, the women linger in the mead;
Treading the green afield, townspeople come and go.

The floating clouds blown off, dim is the distant hill;
Flute-songs are hushed, deserted gardens quiet.
Steeped in pure moonlight, the middle court is still;
Without a shadow, the willow-downs run riot.

Zhang Xian (990—1078) was a statesman-poet well known for his verse "The moon breaks through the clouds, with shadows flowers play." This poem written on Cold Food Day in 1075 depicts the beautiful spring scenes and the tranquil night scene of the Southern land.

浣溪沙[①]

[宋] 晏 殊

一曲新词酒一杯,
去年天气旧亭台,
夕阳西下几时回?

无可奈何花落去,
似曾相识燕归来,
小园香径独徘徊。

[①] 浣溪沙:唐玄宗时教坊曲名,后用为词调。沙,一作"纱"。

Tune: Sand of Silk-washing Stream

Yan Shu

I compose a new song and drink a cup of wine
In the bower of last year when weather is as fine.
When will you come back now the sun's on the decline?

Deeply I sign for the fallen flowers in vain;
Vaguely I seem to know the swallows come again.
Loitering on the garden path, I alone remain.

Yan Shu (991—1055) passed the civil service examinations in his early teens and became prime minister under the reign of Renzong of Song Dynasty (reigned 1022—1063). This poem was written for a beautiful songstress for whom he had composed lyrical songs one year before.

破阵子[1]

[宋] 晏 殊

燕子来时新社[2],
梨花落后清明。
池上碧苔三四点,
叶底黄鹂一两声,
日长飞絮轻。

巧笑[3]东邻女伴,
采桑径里逢迎。
疑怪昨宵春梦好,
原是今朝斗草赢,
笑从双脸生。

---

① 破阵子:唐教坊曲名,又名"十拍子"。
② 新社:春社,立春后第五个戊日。时近清明,古人在此日祭土神祈求丰收,相传燕子会在此时飞来。
③ 巧笑:美好的笑容。

Tune: Dance of the Cavalry

Yan Shu

When swallows come, we worship gods of spring;
Then flowers fall, we mourn for the dear dead.
We hear, amid the leaves, the orioles sing;
Beside the pool we see the green moss spread.
The willow catkins fly as the day's lengthening.

My neighbour's daughter and her friends are sweet,
Mulberry leaves to gather now they meet.
Last night, she wonders, why such happy dreams?
They foretell that she wins the game of grass, it seems.
A sparkling smile upon her fair face beams.

This poem depicts in the first stanza the spring days when country folk worshipped local gods and mourned for their ancestors. In the second we find a vivid description of country lasses gathering mulberry leaves for silkworms and playing the game of one hundred grasses.

离亭燕

[宋]张　昇

一带①江山如画，
风物向秋潇洒。
水浸碧天何处断，
霁色②冷光相射。
蓼屿③荻花洲，
掩映竹篱茅舍。

云际客帆高挂，
烟外酒旗低亚。
多少六朝④兴废事，
尽入渔樵闲话。
怅望倚层楼，
寒日无言西下。

① 一带：指金陵（今南京）一带地区。
② 霁色：雨后初晴的景色。
③ 蓼屿：指长满蓼花的高地。
④ 六朝：指东吴、东晋、宋、齐、梁、陈六个朝代，均在南京一带建都。

Tune: Swallows Leaving Pavilion

Zhang Bian

So picturesque the land by riverside.

In autumn tints the scenery is purified.

Without a break green waves merge into azure sky.

The sunbeams after rain take chilly dye:

Bamboo fence dimly seen 'mid islet reeds

And shoreline thatch-roofed cottages o'ergrown with weeds.

Among white clouds are lost white sails,

And where smoke coils up slow,

There wineshop flag hangs low.

How many of the fisherman's and woodsman's tales

Are told about the Six Dynasties' fall and rise!

Saddened, I lean upon the tower's rails.

Mutely the sun turns cold and sinks in western skies.

Zhang Bian (992—1077) was vice-premier during the reign of Renzong of Song Dynasty (reigned 1022—1063). In this poem he describes the riverside scenery of Jinling (present-day Nanjing), capital of the Six Dynasties (221—261; 317—589). In the second stanza he expresses his feeling towards the vicissitudes of more than 300 years.

生查子

[宋]欧阳修

去年元夜①时,
花市②灯如昼。
月上柳梢头,
人约黄昏后。

今夜元夜时,
月与灯依旧。
不见去年人,
泪湿青衫袖。

① 元夜:农历正月十五夜,即元宵节,也称上元节。
② 花市:繁华的街市。

Tune: Mountain Hawthorn

Ouyang Xiu

Last year on this moonlit spring night,
Lanterns in Flower Fair were bright.
The moon rose above the willow tree,
At dusk he had a tryst with me.

This year on the same moonlit night,
The moon and lanterns are as bright.
Where is my beloved of last year?
My sleeves are wet with tear on tear.

Ouyang Xiu (1007—1072) was the vice-premier who made important contribution to the development of literature during the Northern Song Dynasty (960—1127), but who represented higher achievement in prose than in poetry. This poem depicts a young woman waiting in vain for her beloved on the night of the Spring Moon Festival or Lantern Festival, that is, the 15th day of the first month by the lunar calendar.

蝶恋花

[宋] 欧阳修

庭院深深深几许？
杨柳堆烟，
帘幕无重数。
玉勒①雕鞍②游冶处③，
楼高不见章台④路。

雨横风狂三月暮，
门掩黄昏，
无计留春住。
泪眼问花花不语，
乱红飞过秋千去。

① 玉勒：玉制的马衔。
② 雕鞍：精雕的马鞍。
③ 游冶处：指歌楼妓院。
④ 章台：汉长安街名。

Tune: Butterflies Lingering over Flowers

Ouyang Xiu

Deep, deep the courtyard where he is, so deep
It's veiled by smoke-like willows heap on heap,
By curtain on curtain and screen on screen.
Leaving his saddle and bridle, there he has been
Merry-making. From my tower he can't be seen.

The third month now, the wind and rain are raging late,
At dusk I bar the gate,
But I can't bar in spring.
My tearful eyes ask flowers but they fail to bring
An answer. I see blossoms fall beyond the swing.

The persona in this poem is a young wife complaining that her husband leads a free life in the brothel and leaves her alone at home in view of the raging rain and the falling flowers which can bring her no consolation but pass away with the departing spring. This poem is also included in *The Poetic Works of Feng Yansi*.

桂枝香[①]

金陵怀古

[宋] 王安石

登临送目,

正故国晚秋,

天气初肃。

千里澄江似练,

翠峰如簇。

征帆去棹[②]残阳里,

背西风、

酒旗斜矗。

彩舟云淡,

星河鹭起,

画图难足。

---

① 桂枝香:词牌名,又名"疏帘淡月",首见于此作。
② 棹(zhào):划船的一种工具,形似桨,也可引申为船。

Tune: Fragrance of Laurel Branch

Memories of the Past at Jinling

Wang Anshi

I climb a height

And strain my sight,

Of autumn late 'tis the best time:

The ancient capital looks sublime!

The limpid river, belt like, flows a thousand miles;

Emerald peaks on peaks tower in grandiose styles.

In the declining sun sails come and go;

In west wind wineshop flags fly high and low.

The painted boat

In clouds afloat,

Like stars in Milky Way white egrets fly.

What a picture before the eye!

Wang Anshi (1021—1086) was the premier who carried out reforms under the reign of Shenzong of Song Dynasty (reigned 1067—1085). This poem describes in the first stanza the scenic splendor of Jinling (present-day Nanjing), ancient capital of Six Dynasties (221—280; 317—589). In the second stanza the poet expresses his feeling on thinking of the captive king who was making merry with his dames in the palace hall while the enemy forces came under the walls of his capital.

念往昔,

繁华竞逐,

叹门外楼头,

悲恨相续。

千古凭高对此,

谩嗟荣辱。

六朝旧事随流水,

但寒烟、

衰草凝绿。

至今商女^①,

时时犹唱,

后庭遗曲^②。

---

① 商女：酒楼茶坊的歌女。
② 后庭遗曲：指歌曲《玉树后庭花》，传为陈后主所作，后人将它看成亡国之音。

In days gone by,

For opulence people did vie.

Alas! Shame came on shame beneath the walls,

In palace halls.

Against the rails, in vain I call

O'er ancient kingdoms' rise and fall.

The running water saw Six Dynasties pass;

But I see only chilly mist and withered grass.

E'en now the songstresses still sing

The songs composed by captive king.

南乡子

[宋] 王安石

自古帝王州,
郁郁葱葱①佳气②浮。
四百年来成一梦,
堪愁,
晋代衣冠③成古丘。

绕水恣④行游,
上尽层城更⑤上楼。
往事悠悠君莫问,
回头,
槛外长江空自流⑥。

① 郁郁葱葱:形容草木极为茂盛。
② 佳气:指产生帝王的一种气,这是一种迷信的说法。
③ 晋代衣冠:李白曾在《登金陵凤凰台》一诗中说:"吴宫花草埋幽径,晋代衣冠成古丘。"这里把晋代与吴宫并举,明确地显示出后代诗人对晋朝的向往。
④ 恣:任意地,自由自在地。
⑤ 更:再、又,不止一次地。
⑥ 出自唐代诗人王勃的《滕王阁诗》中的名句:"阁中帝子今何在,槛外长江空自流。"

Tune: Song of a Southern Country

Wang Anshi

The capital was ruled by kings since days gone by.
There rich green and lush gloom breathe a majestic sigh.
Like dreams has passed the reign of four hundred long years,
Which calls forth tears:
Modern laureates are buried like their ancient peers.

Along the river I go where I will,
Up city-walls and watch-towers I gaze my fill.
Do not ask what has passed without leaving a trail!
To what avail?
The endless river rolls in vain beyond the rail.

After the failure of his reforms, Wang Anshi resigned from the premiership and lived in seclusion at Jinling, ancient capital during nearly 400 years (221—280; 317—389; 937—975). In this lyric he gives vent to his discontent about the actual state of things in the court.

卜算子

送鲍浩然之浙东

[宋] 王　观

水是眼波横①,
山是眉峰聚②。
欲问行人去那边?
眉眼盈盈处③。

才始送春归,
又送君归去。
若到江南赶上春,
千万和春住。

① 眼波横：形容眼神闪动，就好像水波横流。
② 眉峰聚：形容双眉蹙皱，就好像两峰并峙。
③ 眉眼盈盈处：比喻山水秀丽的地方。盈盈，美好的样子。

Tune: Song of Divination

Parting with Bao Haoran

Wang Guan

A stretch of rippling water is the beaming eye;

The arched brows around are mountains high.

If you ask where the wayfarer is bound,

Just see where beaming eyes and arched brows are found.

I've just seen spring depart,

And now again with you I'll part.

If you o'ertake in the South the spring day,

Be sure not to let it slip away.

Wang Guan (date uncertain) passed the civil service examinations in 1057. This poem was written for Bao Haoran who was going to the south of the Yangzi River in late spring.

虞美人

有美堂[①] 赠述古

[宋] 苏 轼

湖山信是东南美,

一望弥千里。

使君能得几回来?

便使樽前醉倒更徘徊。

沙河塘[②]里灯初上,

水调谁家唱。

夜阑风静欲归时,

唯有一江明月碧琉璃。

① 有美堂:在杭州城内吴山上,宋仁宗时梅挚所建。
② 沙河塘:在杭州城南,通钱塘江,宋时为杭州繁华地区。

Tune: The Beautiful Lady Yu

Written for Chen Xiang at the Scenic Hall

Su Shi

How fair the lakes and hills of Southern land,
With plains extending as a golden strand!
How oft, wine-cup in hand, have you been here
To make us linger drunk though we appear?

By Sandy River Pond the new-lit lamps are bright.
Who sings "The Water Melody" at night?
When I come back, the wind goes down, the bright moon paves
With emerald glass the river waves.

Su Shi (1037—1101) has been regarded by many as the greatest of poets in Song Dynasty. This poem was written for Chen Xiang, governor of Hangzhou who feasted his subordinate officials in the Scenic Hall built on Mount Wu by the side of the West Lake, before he was going to leave office in 1074.

江城子

密州[①]出猎

[宋] 苏　轼

老夫聊发少年狂,
左牵黄,右擎苍[②],
锦帽貂裘,
千骑卷平岗。
为报倾城随太守,
亲射虎,看孙郎[③]。

酒酣胸胆尚开张。
鬓微霜,又何妨。
持节云中,
何日遣冯唐[④]?
会挽雕弓如满月,
西北望,射天狼。

[①] 密州:在今山东省诸城市。
[②] 左牵黄,右擎苍:左手牵着黄狗,右臂托起苍鹰,形容围猎时用以追捕猎物的架势。
[③] 孙郎:三国时期东吴的孙权,这里作者自喻。
[④] 何日遣冯唐:典出《史记·冯唐列传》。汉文帝时,魏尚为云中(汉时的郡名,在今内蒙古自治区托克托县一带,包括山西西北部分地区)太守。他爱惜士卒,优待军吏,匈奴远避。匈奴曾一度来犯,魏尚亲率车骑出击,所杀甚众。后因报功文书上所载杀敌的数字与实际不合(虚报了六个),被削职。经冯唐代为辨白后,认为判得过重,文帝就派冯唐"持节"(带着传达圣旨的符节)去敕免魏尚的罪,让魏尚仍然担任云中郡太守。苏轼此时因政治上处境不好,调密州太守,故以魏尚自许,希望能得到朝廷的信任。

Tune: A Riverside Town

Hunting at Mizhou

Su Shi

Rejuvenated, I my fiery zeal display:
On left hand leash, a yellow hound,
On right hand wrist, a falcon gray.
A thousand slik-capped, sable-coated horsemen sweep
Across the rising ground
And hillocks steep.
Townspeople pour from out the city gate
To watch the tiger-hunting magistrate.

Heart gladdened with strong wine, who cares
About a few new-frosted hairs?
When will the court imperial send
Me as their envoy? With flags and banners then I'll bend
My bow like a full moon, and aiming northwest, I
Will shoot down the fierce Wolf from out the sky.

This poem was written in 1075 when the poet was magistrate of Mizhou. "The Wolf" here stands for the Qiang tribesmen then fighting with the Hans.

江城子

乙卯正月二十日夜记梦

[宋] 苏 轼

十年①生死两茫茫，
不思量，
自难忘。
千里孤坟，
无处话凄凉。
纵使相逢应不识，
尘满面，
鬓如霜。

夜来幽梦忽还乡，
小轩窗，
正梳妆。
相顾无言，
唯有泪千行。
料得年年肠断处，
明月夜，
短松冈②。

① 十年：指结发妻子王弗去世已十年。
② 短松冈：苏轼葬妻之地。

Tune: A Riverside Town

Dreaming of My Deceased Wife on the Night of the 20th Day of the 1st Month

Su Shi

For ten long years the living of the dead knows nought.
Though to my mind not brought,
Could the dead be forgot?
Her lonely grave is far, a thousand miles away.
To whom can I my grief convey?
Revived, e'en if she be, could she know me?
My face is worn with care
And frosted is my hair.

Last night I dreamed of coming to my native place:
She's making up her face
Before her mirror with grace.
Each saw the other hushed,
But from our eyes tears gushed.
When I am woken, I fancy her heart broken
Each night when the moon shines
O'er her grave clad with pines.

This lyric was written at Mizhou in 1075. The poet dreamed of his first wife, Wang Fu, whom he married in 1054 when she was fifteen. She died in 1065, and the following year, when the poet's father died, he carried her remains back to his old home in Sichuan and buried them in the family plot, planting a number of little pines around the grave mound.

水调歌头

[宋] 苏 轼

丙辰①中秋,欢饮达旦,大醉,作此篇,兼怀子由。

明月几时有?
把酒问青天。
不知天上宫阙,
今夕是何年?
我欲乘风归去,
又恐琼楼玉宇②,
高处不胜③寒。
起舞弄清影,
何似在人间?

---

① 丙辰:指宋神宗熙宁九年(1076)。这一年苏轼在密州(今山东诸城)任太守。
② 琼楼玉宇:美玉砌成的楼宇,指想象中的月宫。
③ 不胜:经不住,承受不了。胜:承担、承受。

Tune: Prelude to the Melody of Water

Su Shi

> On the night of the Mid-autumn Festival of 1076, I drank happily till dawn and wrote this in my cups while thinking of Ziyou.

How long will the bright moon appear?

Wine-cup in hand, I ask the sky.

I do not know what time of year

It would be tonight in the palace on high.

Riding the wind, there I would fly,

Yet I fear the crystal palace would be

Far too high and cold for me.

I rise and dance, with my shadow I play.

On high as on earth, would it be as gay?

This is a famous Midautumn lyric written for his brother Ziyou (1039—1112) when the poet was away from the imperial court. According to some commentators, "the palace on high" might allude to the imperial palace and therefore, after reading this lyric, Shenzong of Song Dynasty said that Su Shi was loyal.

转朱阁,
低绮户①,
照无眠。
不应有恨,
何事长向别时圆?
人有悲欢离合,
月有阴晴圆缺,
此事古难全。
但愿人长久,
千里共婵娟②。

① 绮户:雕饰华丽的门窗。
② 婵娟:本意指妇女姿态美好的样子,这里形容月亮。

The moon goes round the mansion red

Through gauze-draped windows soft to shed

Her light upon the sleepless bed.

Against man she should have no spite.

Why then when people part is she oft full and bright?

Men have sorrow and joy, they part or meet again;

The moon may be bright or dim, she may wax or wane.

There has been nothing perfect since the olden days.

So let us wish that man

Will live long as he can!

Though miles apart, we'll share the beauty she displays.

浣溪沙

[宋]苏 轼

簌簌衣巾落枣花。
村南村北响缫车①。
牛衣②古柳卖黄瓜。

酒困路长惟欲睡,
日高人渴漫思茶③。
敲门试问野人家。

---

① 缫车:纺车。缫,一作"缲",把蚕茧浸在热水里,抽出蚕丝。
② 牛衣:蓑衣之类。这里泛指用粗麻织成的衣服。
③ 漫思茶:想随便去哪儿找点茶喝。

Tune: Sand of Silk-washing Stream

Su Shi

Date-flowers fall in showers on my hooded head,
At both ends of the village wheels are spinning thread,
A straw-cloak'd man sells cucumber beneath a willow tree.

Wine-drowsy when the road is long, I yawn for bed;
Throat parched when sun is high, I long for tea,
I'll knock at this door. What have they for me?

This is one of the five lyrics written in 1078 when Su Shi, magistrate of Xuzhou, went to the Rocky Pool to give thanks for the rain. It presents a rural scene in early summer and shows the cordial relation between the magistrate and villagers.

浣溪沙

[宋] 苏 轼

游蕲水①清泉寺,寺临兰溪,溪水西流。

山下兰芽短浸溪。
松间沙路净无泥。
萧萧暮雨子规啼。

谁道人生无再少②?
门前流水尚能西。
休将白发唱黄鸡。

---

① 蕲(qí)水:县名,今湖北省黄冈市浠水县。
② 无再少:不能回到少年时代。

Tune: Sand of Silk-washing Stream

Su Shi

> I visited the Temple of Clear Fountain on the Stream of Orchid which flows westward.

In the brook below the hill there drowns the orchid bud;
The sandy path between pine-trees shows not a trace of mud.
Shower by shower falls the rain while cuckoos sing.

Who says an old man can't return once more unto his spring?
Before Clear Fountain's temple the water still flows west.
Why can't the cock still crow at dawn though with a snow-white crest?

It was generally believed in China that a river would flow eastward to the sea as naturally as man should grow old. After his convalescence in 1082, the poet visited the west-flowing Stream of Orchid and was confirmed in his conviction that an old man should be optimistic just as an old cock with a white crest should still crow at dawn.

永遇乐

[宋] 苏 轼

彭城夜宿燕子楼①,梦盼盼,因作此词。

明月如霜,

好风如水,

清景无限。

曲港跳鱼,

圆荷泻露,

寂寞无人见。

紞如②三鼓,

铿然③一叶,

黯黯梦云④惊断⑤。

夜茫茫,

重寻无处,

觉来小园行遍。

① 燕子楼:唐代徐州尚书为他的爱妓盼盼所筑的小楼。
② 紞(dǎn)如:击鼓的声音。
③ 铿然:清越的音响。铿然一叶说的是夜深人静,所以听叶落声也觉得是清脆的金石之声。
④ 梦云:夜里梦见神女朝云,这里云指代盼盼。
⑤ 惊断:惊醒。

Tune: Joy of Eternal Union

Su Shi

> I lodged at the Pavilion of Swallows in Pengcheng, dreamed of the fair lady Panpan, and wrote the following lyric.

The bright moonlight is like frost white,

The gentle breeze like water clean:

Far and wide extends the scene serene.

In the haven fish leap

And dew-drops roll down lotus leaves

In solitude no man perceives.

A leaf falls in the night so deep,

Then drums beat thrice with a ring so loud

That gloomy, I awake from my dream of the Cloud.

Under the boundless pall of night,

Nowhere again can she be found

Though I've searched o'er all the small garden's ground.

The Pavilion of Swallows in Pengcheng (present-day Xuzhou) was the place where the fair lady Panpan (referred to as "the Cloud" in this lyric) lived alone for more than ten years, refusing to remarry after the death of her beloved lord.

天涯倦客,

山中归路,

望断故园心眼①。

燕子楼空,

佳人何在?

空锁楼中燕。

古今如梦,

何曾梦觉?

但有旧欢新怨。

异时对、

黄楼②夜景,

为余浩叹。

① 心眼:心愿。
② 黄楼:徐州东门上的大楼,苏轼担任徐州知州时所建。

A tired wanderer far from home
Vainly through mountains and hills may roam,
His native land from view is gone.
The Pavilion of Swallows is empty. Where
Is the lady Panpan so fabled and fair?
The Pavilion shows swallows' nest is draw
Both the past and the present are like dreams
From which we have ne'er been awake, it seems.
We have joys and sorrows both old and new.
Some future day others will come to view
The Yellow Tower's night scenery,
Would they then sigh for me!

西江月

[宋] 苏 轼

> 顷在黄州,春夜行蕲水中,过酒家,饮酒醉,乘月至一溪桥上,解鞍,曲肱醉卧少休。及觉已晓,乱山攒拥,流水锵然,疑非尘世也,书此语桥柱上。

照野弥弥①浅浪,
横空隐隐层霄。
障泥②未解玉骢③骄,
我欲醉眠芳草。

可惜一溪风月,
莫教踏碎琼瑶。
解鞍欹枕绿杨桥,
杜宇④一声春晓。

① 弥弥:水波翻动的样子。
② 障泥:马鞯,垂于马两旁以挡泥土。
③ 玉骢:良马。
④ 杜宇:指杜鹃鸟。

Tune: The Moon over the West River

Su Shi

> On a spring night I passed a wine-shop, drank there and then rode by moonlight to a bridge where I lay down and slept. Awake at dawn, I found the hills in rich green and lush gloom like an earthly paradise, and wrote down this lyric on the bridge.

Wave on wave glimmers by the river shores;

Sphere on sphere dimly appears in the sky.

Unsaddled now is my white-jade-like horse.

Drunken, asleep in the sweet grass I'll lie.

My horse's hoofs may break, I'm afraid,

The breeze-rippled brook paved by moon light's white jade,

I tie fast my horse to a bough of green willow

Near the bridge then I pillow

My head on saddle and sleep till the cuckoo's songs awake

A spring daybreak.

This lyric was written at Huangzhou in 1082.

定风波

[宋] 苏 轼

> 三月七日沙湖①道中遇雨,雨具先去,同行皆狼狈,余独不觉。已而遂晴,故作此。

莫听穿林打叶声。

何妨吟啸且徐行。

竹杖芒鞋②轻胜马,

谁怕!

一蓑③烟雨任平生。

料峭春风吹酒醒,

微冷。

山头斜照却相迎。

回首向来萧瑟处,

归去,

也无风雨也无晴。

① 沙湖:在今湖北黄冈东南三十里,又名螺丝店。
② 芒鞋:草鞋。
③ 蓑(suō):蓑衣,用棕制成的雨披。

Tune: Calming the Waves

Su Shi

On the 7th day of the 3rd month we were caught in rain on our way to the Sandy Lake. The umbrellas had gone ahead, my companions were quite downhearted, but I took no notice. It soon cleared, and I wrote this.

Listen not to the rain beating against the trees.
Why don't you slowly walk and chant at ease?
Better than a saddle I like sandals and cane.
I'd fain,
In a straw cloak, spend my life in mist and rain.

Drunken, I am sobered by the vernal wind shrill
And rather chill.
In front, I see the slanting sun atop the hill;
Turning my head, I see the dreary beaten track.
Let me go back!
Impervious to rain or shine, I'll have my own will.

Su Shi wrote this lyric on his way back from the Sandy Lake, fifteen kilometers to the east of Huangzhou where he had been banished since 1080.

念奴娇

赤壁[①]怀古

[宋] 苏 轼

大江[②]东去,
浪淘尽千古风流人物。
故垒[③]西边,
人道是三国周郎[④]赤壁。
乱石穿空,
惊涛拍岸,
卷起千堆雪。
江山如画,
一时多少豪杰。

① 赤壁:此指黄州赤壁,在今湖北黄冈西。
② 大江:指长江。
③ 故垒:过去遗留下来的营垒。
④ 周郎:指三国时吴国名将周瑜。

Tune: Charm of a Maiden Singer

Memories of the Past at Red Cliff

Su Shi

The Great River eastward flows,

With its waves are gone all those

Gallant heroes of bygone years.

West of the ancient fortress appears

The Red Cliff. Here General Zhou won his early fame

When the Three Kingdoms were all in flame.

Jagged rocks tower in the air,

Swashing waves beat on the shore,

Rolling up a thousand heaps of snow.

To match the hills and the river so fair,

How many heroes brave of yore

Made a great show!

This is a Su Shi's famous lyric written at Red Cliff where General Zhou Yu defeated the enemy advancing forces in AD 208.

遥想公瑾当年,

小乔初嫁了,

雄姿英发[①]。

羽扇纶巾[②],

谈笑间,

樯橹[③]灰飞烟灭。

故国神游,

多情应笑我,

早生华发。

人生如梦,

一尊还酹江月。

[①] 英发：谈吐不凡，见识卓越。
[②] 纶巾：青丝制成的头巾。
[③] 樯橹：这里代指曹操的水军战船。樯，挂帆的桅杆。橹，一种摇船的桨。

I fancy General Zhou at the height

Of his success, with a plume fan in hand,

In a silk hood, so brave and bright,

Laughing and jesting with his bride so fair,

While enemy ships were destroyed as planned

Like shadowy castles in the air.

Should their souls revisit this land,

Sentimental, his wife would laugh to say,

Younger than they, I have my hair all turned gray.

Life is but like a passing dream,

I'd drink to the moon which once saw them on the stream.

临江仙

夜归临皋

[宋] 苏 轼

夜饮东坡[①]醒复醉,
归来仿佛三更。
家童鼻息已雷鸣。
敲门都不应,
倚杖听江声。

长恨此身非我有,
何时忘却营营[②]?
夜阑风静縠纹[③]平。
小舟从此逝,
江海寄余生。

---

① 东坡:在湖北省黄冈市东。
② 营营:周旋、忙碌。
③ 縠(hú)纹:比喻水波细纹。縠,绉纱类丝织品。

Tune: Immortal at the River

Returning to Lingao by Night

Su Shi

Drinking at Eastern Slope by night,
I sober, then get drunk again.
When I come back, it's near midnight.
I hear the thunder of my houseboy's snore,
I knock but no one answers at my door.
What can I do but, leaning on my cane,
Listen to the river's refrain?

I long regret I am not master of my own.
When can I just ignore the hums of up and down?
In the still night the soft winds quiver
On the ripples of the river.
From now on, I would vanish with my little boat,
For the rest of my life, on the sea I would float.

Because of the last two lines, it is said, a rumor spread around that the poet had actually gotten into a boat in the night and disappeared. The governor of Huangzhou, who was responsible for seeing that Su Shi did not leave the district, rushed in alarm to the poet's house, to find him in bed snoring. Word of his supposed escape even reached Shenzong of Song Dynasty in the capital.

水龙吟

次韵章质夫杨花词

[宋]苏 轼

似花还似非花,

也无人惜从教坠。

抛家傍路,

思量却是,

无情有思①。

萦损柔肠,

困酣娇眼②,

欲开还闭。

梦随风万里,

寻郎去处,

又还被,

莺呼起。

① 无情有思（sì）：杨花看似无情，却自有它的愁思。
② 娇眼：美人娇媚的眼睛，比喻柳叶。古人诗赋中常称初生的柳叶为柳眼。

Tune: Water Dragon Chant

After Zhang Zhifu's lyric on willow catkins, using the same rhyming words.

Su Shi

They seem to be yet not be flowers,
None pity them when they fall down in showers.
Forsaking home,
By the roadside they roam;
I think they have no feeling to impart,
But they could have thoughts deep.
See grief benumb their tender heart,
Their wistful eyes near shut with sleep,
About to open, yet closed again.
They dream of going with the wind for long,
Long miles to find a tender-hearted man,
But are aroused by the orioles' song.

This poem written after Zhang Zhifu's lyric is generally acknowledged to be better than the original, for Su Shi personifies willow catkins as a lonely woman longing for her husband. The "orioles' song" refers to the following Tang poem:

> *Drive orioles off the tree*
> *For their songs awake me*
> *From dreaming of my dear*
> *Far off on the frontier.*

According to Su Shi's own note, "it is said that when willow catkins fall into the water, they turn into duckweed." This is of course the poet's imagination.

不恨此花飞尽,
恨西园落红难缀。
晓来雨过,
遗踪何在?
一池萍碎。
春色①三分,
二分尘土,
一分流水。
细看来不是杨花,
点点是离人泪。

① 春色：代指杨花。

I do not grieve the willow catkins flown away,
But that in Western Garden fallen red
Can't be restored. When dawns the day
And rain is o'er, we cannot find their traces
But in a pond with duckweeds overspread.
Of Spring's three graces,
Two have gone with the roadside dust;
One with the waves. But if you just
Take a close look, you will never
Find catkins but tear-drops of those who sever.

蝶恋花

[宋] 苏 轼

花褪[①]残红青杏小。
燕子飞时,
绿水人家绕。
枝上柳绵吹又少。
天涯何处无芳草。

墙里秋千墙外道。
墙外行人,
墙里佳人笑。
笑渐不闻声渐悄。
多情却被无情恼。

① 褪:脱去。

Tune: Butterflies Lingering over Flowers

Su Shi

Red flowers fade, green apricots still small
When swallows pass
Over blue water which surrounds the garden wall.
Most willow catkins have been blown away, alas!
But there is no place where grows not the sweet green grass.

Without the wall there's a road; within there's a swing.
A passer-by
Hears a fair maiden's laughter in the garden ring.
As the ringing laughter dies away by and by,
For the enchantress the enchant'd can only sigh.

This lyric is supposed to have been written while the poet was banished to Hainan Island, southernmost part of the Song territory. The first stanza describes the departing spring and the second depicts the sorrow of a wayfarer far from home.

卜算子

[宋] 李之仪

我住长江头,
君住长江尾。
日日思君不见君,
共饮长江水。

此水几时休,
此恨何时已①。
只愿君心似我心,
定不负相思意。

① 已:完结,停止。

Tune: Song of Divination

Li Zhiyi

I live upstream and you

Downstream by River Blue.

Day after day of you I think,

But you are not in view,

Although as one we drink

The water clear of River Blue.

When will the water no more flow?

When will my grief no longer grow?

I wish your heart be but like mine,

Then not in vain for you I pine.

Li Zhiyi (1038—1117) passed the civil service examinations in 1070. He wrote a lyric to the tune of Dream of A Maid of Honor, using the same rhyming words as Li Bai's, which shows the fourth lyric in this anthology was regarded as Li Bai's as early as the Northern Song Dynasty. The persona in this Song of Divination is a young woman longing to see her beloved one.

清平乐

晚春

[宋]黄庭坚

春归何处?
寂寞无行路①。
若有人知春去处,
唤取归来同住。

春无踪迹谁知,
除非问取②黄鹂③。
百啭④无人能解,
因风⑤飞过蔷薇。

① 无行路:没有可供游玩的地方,这里指春天没有留下回去的踪迹。
② 问取:问。
③ 黄鹂:鸟名,又叫黄莺,每到春天才叫,声音婉转动听。
④ 啭:鸟鸣。
⑤ 因风:趁着风势。

Tune: Pure Serene Music

Late Spring

Huang Tingjian

Where has Spring gone?
No trace is left on pathway lone.
If you know where she is today,
Please call her back to stay.

Who can find traceless Spring?
Unless you ask the orioles which sing
A hundred tunes none understand.
Riding the wind, they fly past rose-grown land.

Huang Tingjian (1045—1105) was one of the followers of Su Shi. This lyric reveals his love of Spring.

鹊桥仙

[宋] 秦 观

纤云①弄巧,
飞星②传恨,
银汉③迢迢暗渡。
金风玉露一相逢,
便胜却人间无数。

柔情似水,
佳期如梦,
忍顾④鹊桥归路。
两情若是久长时,
又岂在朝朝暮暮!

---

① 纤云:轻盈的云彩。
② 飞星:流星。一说指牵牛、织女二星。
③ 银汉:指银河。
④ 忍顾:怎忍回头看。

Tune: Immortal at the Magpie Bridge

Qin Guan

Clouds float like works of art;
Stars shoot with grief at heart.
Across the Milky Way the Cowherd meets the Maid.
When autumn's Golden Wind embraces Dew of Jade,
All the love scenes on earth, however many, fade.

Their tender love flows like a stream;
This happy date seems but a dream.
Can they bear a separate homeward way?
If love between both sides can last for aye,
Why need they stay together night and day?

Qin Guan (1049—1100) was another follower of Su Shi. This lyric eclipsed all other love poems by versifying the old legend concerning the Cowherd and the Maid or the Weaver, two starts separated by the Milky Way, who were to meet across a magpie bridge once every year on the 7th day of the 7th lunar month when the golden autumn wind embraced the dew impearled like jade.

踏莎行

郴州①旅舍

[宋] 秦 观

雾失楼台,
月迷津渡,
桃源望断无寻处。
可堪②孤馆闭春寒,
杜鹃声里斜阳暮。

驿寄梅花,
鱼传尺素③,
砌成此恨无重数。
郴江幸自绕郴山,
为谁流下潇湘去?

① 郴(chēn)州:今属湖南。
② 可堪:怎堪,受不住。
③ 鱼传尺素:古时舟车劳顿,信件很容易损坏,古人便将信件放入鱼形匣子中,美观而又方便携带。尺素:小幅的丝织物,如绢、帛等。指书信。

Tune: Treading on Grass

At an Inn of Chenzhou

Qin Guan

The bowers lost in mist,

Dimmed ferry in moonlight,

Peach Blossom Land ideal beyond the sight.

Shut up in lonely inn, can I bear the cold spring?

I hear at lengthening sunset the home-bound cuckoos sing.

Mume blossoms sent by friends

And letters brought by post,

Nostalgic thoughts uncounted assail me oft in host.

The local river flows around the local hill.

Should it flow to foreign lands and flow against its will?

This lyric was written in 1097 when the poet was banished to Chenzhou. The Peach Blossom Land was the Utopia for Chinese literati.

捣练子

[宋] 贺　铸

砧①面莹②,
杵③声齐,
捣就④征衣⑤泪墨题⑥。
寄到玉关应万里⑦,
戍人⑧犹在玉关西。

① 砧(zhēn):垫在下面捶衣服的石头。
② 莹:光洁,光亮。
③ 杵:捶衣服的木棒。
④ 捣就:捶完。
⑤ 征衣:出征军人的衣服。
⑥ 泪墨题:泪水和着墨汁题写征衣的包封。
⑦ 应万里:应该有万里之遥。
⑧ 戍人:指正在戍守边疆的丈夫。

Tune: Song of Broken Chains

He Zhu

Regularly the beetle sounds
As on the anvil stone it pounds.
After washing her warrior's dress,
With ink and tears she writes down his address.
The package goes a thousand miles to the Jade Pass,
But the warrior is stationed farther west, alas!

He Zhu (1052—1125) was also a follower of Su Shi. This lyric depicts a washerwoman sending winter garments to her husband stationed in a garrison town farther west than the Jade Pass on the northwestern frontier.

鹧鸪天

[宋] 贺 铸

重过阊门①万事非,
同来何事②不同归③。
梧桐半死④清霜后⑤,
头白鸳鸯失伴飞。

原上草,
露初晞⑥,
旧栖⑦新垅⑧两依依。
空床卧听南窗雨,
谁复挑灯夜补衣?

① 阊(chāng)门:苏州城的西门叫阊门,这里指代苏州。
② 何事:为什么,为何。
③ 不同归:作者夫妇曾居住过苏州,后来妻子死去,他一人独自离去,所以说是不同归。
④ 梧桐半死:据说用半死梧桐的根制作出来的琴,声音最悲,这里用来比喻自己遭丧偶之痛。
⑤ 清霜后:秋天,这里指年老。
⑥ 露初晞:这里诗人把短暂的人生比作早晨的露水,形容人生极其短促。晞,干燥。
⑦ 旧栖:旧居,指生者所居处。
⑧ 新垅:新坟,指死者葬所。

Tune: The Partridge Sky

He Zhu

All things have changed. Once more I pass the Gate.

We came together, I go back without my mate.

Bitten by hoary frost, half the parasol dies;

Life-long companion lost, one lonely love-bird flies.

Grass wet with dew

Dries on the plain,

How can I leave our old abode and her grave new!

Lying in half empty bed, I hear the pelting rain.

Who will turn up the wick to mend my coat again?

This is an elegy written in memory of the poet's wife who lived together with the poet near the city gate of Suzhou, died in their abode and was buried in the graveyard.

苏幕遮

[宋]周邦彦

燎①沉香,
消溽暑②。
鸟雀呼晴,
侵晓窥檐语。
叶上初阳干宿雨
水面清圆,
一一风荷举。

故乡遥,
何日去?
家住吴门③,
久作长安旅。
五月渔郎相忆否?
小楫轻舟,
梦入芙蓉浦④。

① 燎(liáo):小火烧炙。
② 溽(rù)暑:夏天闷热潮湿的暑气。溽,湿润潮湿。
③ 吴门:古吴县城亦称吴门,即今之江苏苏州。作者是钱塘人,钱塘古属吴郡,故称之。
④ 浦:水湾、河流。

Tune: Screened by Southern Curtain

Zhou Bangyan

I burn an incense sweet
To temper steamy heat.
Birds chirp at dawn beneath the eaves,
Announcing a fine day. The rising sun
Has dried last night's raindrops on lotus leaves
Which, clear and round, dot water surface. One by one
The lotus blooms stand up with ease
And swing in morning breeze.

My homeland is far away,
When may I return to stay?
My kinsfolk live in South by city wall.
Why should I stay long in the capital?
Will not my fishing friends remember me in May?
In a short-oared light boat, it seems,
I'm back 'mid lotus blooms in dreams.

Zhou Bangyan (1057—1121), a court musician and poet skilled in the composition of "slow tunes", has created a number of new patterns. This lyric describes in the first stanza a summer morning in the capital, and the second stanza expresses the poet's longing for his homeland in the South.

蝶恋花

早行

[宋]周邦彦

月皎惊乌栖不定,
更漏①将残,
辘轳②牵金井③。
唤起两眸清炯炯④。
泪花落枕红绵冷。

执手霜风吹鬓影,
去意徊徨,
别语愁难听。
楼上阑干⑤横斗柄⑥,
露寒人远鸡相应。

① 更漏:古代的时候看刻漏来报更,所以称刻漏为更漏,常指夜晚之时。
② 辘(lù)轳:井上的汲水器。
③ 金井:井的美称。
④ 炯炯:明亮闪光的样子。
⑤ 阑干:横斜的样子。
⑥ 斗柄:北斗七星的第五至第七的三颗星像古代酌酒所用的斗把,叫作斗柄。

Tune: Butterflies Lingering over Flowers

Parting in the Early Morning

Zhou Bangyan

The crow feels restless, startled by moonlight,

The waterclock drips out as later grows the night,

The windlass lifts water from the well painted gold.

She wakes me with her beaming eyes so bright,

I find the pillow wet with tears and cold.

I take her hand in mine when the frosty wind blows

And her soft-lift hair on her forehead flows.

I'm loath to leave

But it will further grieve

To hear her bid adieu.

She can see from upstairs the stars' Plough in the sky

While I am far away, my mantle damp with dew,

And hear cocks' crow arouse some echoes far and nigh.

This lyric depicts the scenes before, during, and after the parting of a husband from his wife.

相见欢

[宋]朱敦儒

金陵^①城上西楼^②,

倚清秋。

万里夕阳垂地,

大江流。

中原乱^③,

簪缨散^④,

几时收?

试倩^⑤悲风吹泪,

过扬州^⑥。

① 金陵:现在的南京市。
② 西楼:一般泛指高楼,李煜《乌夜啼》有:"无言独上西楼,月如钩。"这里指南京的城楼。
③ 中原乱:指1127年,金兵南侵,汴京陷落,徽、钦二帝被掳北上事。
④ 簪缨散:指仕宦冠服,这里借指仕族逃散流亡。
⑤ 倩:通"请"。
⑥ 扬州:当时处于宋金对峙前方,屡受金兵进犯,建炎三年(1129)几乎被焚烧破坏殆尽。

Tune: Joy at Meeting

Zhu Dunru

I lean on western railings on the city wall
Of Jinling in the fall.
Shedding its rays o'er miles and miles, the sun hangs low
To see the great River flow.

The Central Plain is in a mess,
Officials disperse in distress.
When to recover our frontiers?
I ask sad winds to blow over Yangzhou my tears.

Zhu Dunru (1081—1159), a native of Luoyang, left the Central Plain occupied by Jurchen invaders for Jinling (present-day Nanjing) in the South. This lyric expressed his sorrow at the sight of the setting sun shedding its rays on the riverside Yangzhou overrun by Jurchen aggressors.

如梦令

[宋] 李清照

昨夜雨疏风骤①,
浓睡②不消残酒③。
试问卷帘人④,
却道海棠依旧。
知否,知否?
应是绿肥红瘦⑤。

① 雨疏风骤:雨点稀疏,风声急骤。
② 浓睡:沉睡。
③ 残酒:残留的酒意。
④ 卷帘人:这里指侍女。
⑤ 绿肥红瘦:绿叶茂盛而红花稀少。

Tune: Like A Dream

Li Qingzhao

Last night the wind was strong and rain was fine,

Sound sleep did not dispel the taste of wine.

I ask the maid who's rolling up the screen.

"The same crabapple tree," she says, "is seen."

"Don't you know,

Don't you know

The red should languish and the green must grow?"

Li Qingzhao (1084—1151) was the most famous poetess of the Song Dynasty. This lyric revealing her love of spring flowers reminds us of a Tang poet's *Spring Morning*:

> *This morn of spring in bed I'm lying,*
> *Not to awake till birds are crying.*
> *After one night of wind and showers,*
> *How many are the fallen flowers!*

一剪梅

[宋] 李清照

红藕香残玉簟①秋。
轻解罗裳,
独上兰舟②。
云中谁寄锦书③来?
雁字回时,
月满西楼。

花自飘零水自流。
一种相思,
两处闲愁。
此情无计可消除,
才下眉头,
却上心头。

① 玉簟(diàn):光滑如玉的竹席。
② 兰舟:船的美称。
③ 锦书:书信的美称。

Tune: A Twig of Mume Blossoms

Li Qingzhao

The jade-like mat feels autumn's cold, I change a coat

And 'mid the fading fragrance

Of lotus pink alone I boat.

Will wild returning geese bring letters through the cloud?

When they come, with moonbeams

My west chamber's o'erflowed.

As water flows and flowers fall without leaving traces,

One and the same longing

O'erflows two lonely places.

I cannot get rid of this sorrow: kept apart

From my eyebrows,

It gnaws my heart.

This lyric depicts the loneliness of the poetess longing for messages from her husband who was far away. The last three lines may be compared with Fan Zhongyan's verse:

> *Such sorrow as appears*
> *On the brows or the heart*
> *Cannot be put apart.*

醉花阴

九日

[宋]李清照

薄雾浓云愁永昼,
瑞脑消金兽①。
佳节又重阳,
玉枕纱橱,
半夜凉初透。

东篱把酒黄昏后,
有暗香盈袖。
莫道不消魂,
帘卷西风,
人比黄花②瘦!

① 瑞脑:一种薰香名。消金兽:香炉里香料逐渐燃尽。金兽:兽形的铜香炉。
② 黄花:指菊花。

Tune: Tipsy in the Flower's Shade

The Double Ninth Festival

Li Qingzhao

In thin mist and thick cloud of incense, sad I stay.
The animal-shaped censer I see all day.
The Double Ninth Festival comes again.
Still alone I remain
In the curtain of gauze, on a pillow of jade,
Which the midnight chill begins to invade.

After dusk I drink wine by East Hedge in full bloom,
My sleeves filled with fragrance and gloom.
Say not my soul
Is not consumed! Should the west wind uproll
The curtain of my bower,
'Twould show a thinner face than yellow flower.

The Double Ninth Festival was the 9th day of the 9th lunar month, Mountain Climbing Day, according to Chinese custom. This lyric depicts how the poetess passed that day from morning till night, her soul consumed by her separation from her husband.

渔家傲

记梦

[宋] 李清照

天接云涛连晓雾,

星河欲转千帆舞。

仿佛梦魂归帝所[①],

闻天语,

殷勤问我归何处。

我报路长嗟日暮,

学诗漫有[②]惊人句。

九万里[③]风鹏正举。

风休住,

蓬舟吹取三山[④]去。

① 帝所:天帝居住的地方。
② 漫有:白白有。
③ 九万里:《庄子·逍遥游》中说鲲鹏飞时扶摇直上九万里之高。
④ 三山:指传说渤海之中有蓬莱、方丈、瀛洲三座仙山。

Tune: Pride of Fishermen

A Dream

Li Qingzhao

Morning mist and surging clouds spread to join the sky,

The Milky Way fades, a thousand sails dance on high.

It seems as if my soul to God's abode would fly,

And l

Be kindly asked where I'm going. I reply:

"The road is long, alas! the sun on the decline,

In vain I'm famed for clever poetical line.

The roc soars up to ninety thousand miles and nine.

O wind mine!

Don't stop but carry my boat to three isles divine!"

This is a manly poem written by a woman poet who dreamed of sailing through the mist, the clouds, the Milky Way and up to God's abode and soaring like the roc on the wing of the wind to the three divine isles ninety thousand li away.

凤凰台上忆吹箫

[宋]李清照

香冷金猊[①],

被翻红浪[②],

起来慵自梳头。

任宝奁[③]尘满,

日上帘钩。

生怕离怀别苦,

多少事,

欲说还休。

新来瘦,

非干病酒,

不是悲秋。

① 金猊(ní):涂金的狮形香炉。
② 红浪:红色被铺乱摊在床上,有如波浪。
③ 宝奁(lián):华贵的梳妆镜匣。

Tune: Playing Flute Recalled on Phoenix Terrace

Li Qingzhao

Incense in gold

Censer is cold,

Quilt on the bed

Spreads like waves red.

I get up, but still weary, I won't comb my hair,

Dressing table undusted, I leave it there.

Now the sun hangs on the drapery's hook.

I'm afraid to recall your parting look.

I've much to say, yet pause as soon as I begin.

Recently I've grown thin,

Not that I'm sick with wine,

Not that for autumn sad I pine.

This is a lyric depicting the poetess longing for her husband who was far away from home.

休休,

这回去也,

千万遍阳关①,

也则难留。

念武陵人远②,

烟锁秦楼。

唯有楼前流水,

应念我、

终日凝眸③。

凝眸处,

从今又添一段新愁。

① 阳关:语出《阳关三叠》,是唐宋时的送别曲。
② 武陵人远:引用陶渊明《桃花源记》中,武陵渔人误入桃花源,离开后再去便找不到路径了。
③ 凝眸:注视。

Be done! be done!

Once you are gone,

No matter what parting songs sing we anew,

We can't keep you.

Far, far away you pass your days;

My bower here is drowned in haze.

In front there is a running brook

Which could never forget my longing look.

From now on, where

I gaze all day long with a vacant stare,

A new grief will grow there.

声声慢

[宋] 李清照

寻寻觅觅,

冷冷清清,

凄凄惨惨戚戚。

乍暖还寒① 时候,

最难将息。

三杯两盏淡酒,

怎敌他、

晚来风急!

雁过也,

正伤心,

却是旧时相识。

① 乍暖还(huán)寒:指秋天的天气,忽然变暖,又转寒冷。

Tune: Slow, Slow Tune

Li Qingzhao

I look for what I miss,

I know not what it is:

I feel so sad, so drear,

So lonely, without cheer.

How hard is it

To keep me fit

In this lingering cold!

Hardly warmed up

By cup on cup

Of wine so dry.

Oh! How could I

Endure at dusk the drift

Of wind so swift?

It breaks my heart, alas!

To see the wild geese pass,

For they are my acquaintances of old.

This famous lyric depicts the loneliness of the poetess after the death of her husband.

满地黄花堆积,

憔悴损,

如今有谁堪摘?

守着窗儿,

独自怎生得黑!

梧桐更兼细雨,

到黄昏、

点点滴滴。

这次第①,

怎一个愁字了得!

---

① 次第:光景,情形。

The ground is covered with yellow flowers

Faded and fallen in showers.

Who will pick them up now?

Sitting alone at the window, how

Could I but quicken

The pace of darkness which won't thicken?

On parasol-trees a fine rain drizzles

As twilight grizzles.

Oh! What can I do with a grief

Beyond belief!

永遇乐

[宋]李清照

落日熔金,
暮云合璧,
人在何处?
染柳烟浓,
吹梅笛怨,
春意知几许?
元宵佳节,
融和天气,
次第岂无风雨?
来相召,
香车宝马①,
谢他酒朋诗侣。

① 香车宝马:这里指贵族妇女所乘坐的、雕镂工致装饰华美的车驾。

Tune: Joy of Eternal Union

Li Qingzhao

The setting sun like molten gold,

Gathering clouds like marble cold,

Where is my dear?

Willows take misty dye,

Flutes for mume blossoms sigh.

Can you say spring is here?

On the Lantern Festival

The weather is agreeable.

Will wind and rain not come again?

I thank my friends in verse and wine,

With scented cabs and horses fine

Coming to invite me in vain.

This lyric was written on a Lantern Festival, the 15th day of the 1st lunar month, after the Jurchen invasion. The poetess thought of the pleasure enjoyed in the lost capital and felt grieved over the death of her dear husband.

中州^①盛日,

闺门多暇,

记得偏重三五^②。

铺翠冠儿,

捻金雪柳^③,

簇带争济楚。

如今憔悴,

风鬟雾鬓^④,

怕见夜间出去。

不如向帘儿底下,

听人笑语。

---

① 中州:即中土、中原。这里指北宋的都城汴京(今河南开封)。
② 三五:十五日。此处指元宵节。
③ 雪柳:雪白如柳叶的头饰。
④ 风鬟雾鬓:发髻蓬乱。指无心打扮。

I remember the pleasure

Ladies enjoyed at leisure

In the capital on this day:

Headdress with emerald

And filigree of gold

Vied in fashion display.

Now with a languid air

And dishevelled frosty hair,

I dare not go out in the evening.

I'd rather forward lean

Behind the window screen

To hear the others' laughter ring.

临江仙

夜登小阁忆洛中旧游

[宋] 陈与义

忆昔午桥①桥上饮,
坐中多是豪英。
长沟流月去无声。
杏花疏影里,
吹笛到天明。

二十余年如一梦,
此身虽在堪惊。
闲登小阁看新晴。
古今多少事,
渔唱②起三更。

---

① 午桥:在洛阳南面。
② 渔唱:打鱼人编的歌谣。

Tune: Immortal at the River

Mounting a Tower at Night and Recalling the Old Friends Visiting Luoyang Together

Chen Yuyi

I still remember drinking on the Bridge of Noon

With bright wits of the day.

The silent moon

On endless river rolled away.

In shadows sparse of apricot flowers

We played our flutes till morning hours.

O'er twenty years have passed like dreams,

It is a wonder that I'm still alive.

Carefree, I mount the tower bathed in moonbeams.

So many things passed long

Ago survive

Only in fishermen's midnight song.

Chen Yuyi (1090—1138) was a native of Luoyang who fled to the South after the Jurchen invasion. The Bridge of Noon was a scenic spot in the south of Luoyang where a villa was built by an official of the Tang Dynasty.

贺新郎

送胡邦衡谪新州

[宋]张元干

梦绕神州路。

怅秋风、

连营画角①,

故宫离黍②。

底事昆仑倾砥柱,

九地黄流乱注?

聚万落千村狐兔。

天意从来高难问,

况人情老易悲难诉,

更南浦,

送君去。

---

① 画角:一种管乐器。传自西羌。形如竹筒,本细末大,以竹木或皮革等制成,因表面有彩绘,故称。发声哀厉高亢,古时军中多用以警昏晓,振士气,肃军容。帝王出巡,亦用以报警戒严。
② 故宫:指汴京旧宫。离黍:亡国之悲。

Tune: Congratulating the Bridegroom

Seeing His Excellence Hu Quan Banished to the South

Zhang Yuangan

Haunted by dreams of the lost Central Plain,

I hear the autumn wind complain.

From tent to tent horns dreary blow;

In ancient palace weeds o'ergrow.

How could Mount Pillar suddenly fall down?

And Yellow River flow throughout the town?

A thousand villages o'errun with foxes and hares?

We can't question the Heaven high,

The court will soon forget embarrassing affairs.

'Tis sad and drear

To say goodbye

At Southern Pier!

Zhang Yuangan (1091—1170) was a patriotic poet of the Southern Song Dynasty (1127—1279). This lyric was written for Hu Quan, a high offcial opposing the capitulationist Premier Qin Gui, who banished him in 1142 to the southernmost place where even the wild geese carrying messages were not supposed to go. In this lyric "Mount Pillar" alludes to the Royal Court, the "Heaven" to the emperor, and "foxes and hares" to the Jurchen aggressors.

凉生岸柳催残暑。

耿斜河,

疏星淡月,

断云微度。

万里江山知何处?

回首对床夜语。

雁不到,

书成谁与?

目尽青天怀今古,

肯儿曹恩怨相尔汝。

举大白^①,

听金缕^②。

---

① 大白:酒杯。
② 金缕:即《金缕曲》,指此词。

Cold breath of river willows flies away

The remnant of a summer day.

The Milky Way slants low,

Past pale moon and sparse stars clouds slowly go.

Mountains and rivers stretch out of view.

Oh! Where shall I find you?

I still remember our talking at dead

Of night while we two lay in bed.

But now wild geese can't go so far.

Who will send my letter there where you are?

I gaze on the blue sky,

Thinking of the hard times gone by.

Can we have but personal love or hate

As beardless young men often state?

Hold up a cup of wine

And hear this song of mine!

满江红

[宋]岳 飞

怒发冲冠[1],
凭阑处、
潇潇雨歇。
抬望眼,
仰天长啸,
壮怀激烈。
三十功名尘与土,
八千里路云和月。
莫等闲、
白了少年头,
空悲切。

---

[1] 怒发(fà)冲冠:气得头发竖起,将帽子顶起。形容十分愤怒。

Tune: The River All Red

Yue Fei

Wraths sets on end my hair,

I lean on railings where

I see the drizzling rain has ceased.

Raising my eyes

Towards the skies,

I heave long sighs,

My wrath not yet appeased.

To dust is gone the fame achieved in thirty years;

Like cloud-veiled moon the thousand-mile land disappears.

Should youthful heads in vain turn gray,

We would regret for aye.

Yue Fei (1103—1141) was a famous patriotic general who repelled the Jurchen invasion in order to recapture the lost thousand li land. This well-known lyric has an inspiriting and invigorating influence on the Chinese people.

靖康耻①,

犹未雪;

臣子恨,

何时灭。

驾长车、

踏破贺兰山②缺。

壮志饥餐胡虏③肉,

笑谈渴饮匈奴④血。

待从头、

收拾旧山河,

朝天阙⑤。

① 靖康耻:宋钦宗靖康二年(1127),金兵攻陷汴京,虏走徽、钦二帝。
② 贺兰山:贺兰山脉,位于宁夏回族自治区与内蒙古自治区交界处,当时被金兵占领。一说是位于河北省邯郸市磁县境内的贺兰山。
③ 胡虏:对女真贵族入侵者的蔑称。
④ 匈奴:古代北方民族之一,这里指金入侵者。
⑤ 天阙:本指宫殿前的楼观,此指皇帝居住的地方。

Our emperors captured,
It is a burning shame.
How could we generals
Quench our vengeful flame!
Driving our chariots of war, we'd go
To cut through our relentless foe.
Valiantly we'd cut off each head;
Laughing, we'd drink the blood they shed.
When we've reconquered our lost land,
In triumph would return our army grand.

满江红

登黄鹤楼有感

[宋] 岳 飞

遥望中原,

荒烟外,

许多城郭。

想当年,

花遮柳护,

凤楼龙阁。

万岁山[①]前珠翠绕,

蓬壶[②]殿里笙歌作。

到而今,

铁骑满郊畿,

风尘恶。

① 万岁山:宋徽宗政和四年(1122年)建于汴京东北角,为皇帝游玩享乐之地。
② 蓬壶:蓬莱,是古代传说中的渤海中三个仙山之一。

Tune: The River All Red

On Mounting Yellow Crane Tower

Yue Fei

I gaze on Central Plain from afar.

Beyond the wasteland drear and dry,

How many cities and towns there are!

In years gone by,

As many pavilions and bowers

Were screened by green willows and red flowers,

The Royal Hill adorned with pearls and emerald,

The Fairy Palace filled with flute songs. Now behold!

'Neath city walls enemy horses raise a dust

When the wind blows in gust.

This is a newly discovered lyric written by Yue Fei in 1138 when he stationed his army in Yuezhou (present-day Wuhan), awaiting orders to reconquer the lost Central Plain. The Yellow Crane Tower was a scenic spot by the side of the Yangzi River, and a Tang poet ascending the Tower wrote the following poem:

> *The sage on yellow crane was gone amid clouds white.*
> *To what avail is Yellow Crane Tower left here?*
> *Once gone, the yellow crane will ne'er on earth alight;*
> *Only white clouds still float in vain from year to year.*
> *By sun-lit river trees can be count'd one by one;*
> *On Parrot Islet sweet grass grows fast and thick.*
> *Where is my native land beyond the setting sun?*
> *The mist-veiled waves of Han River make me homesick.*

兵安在?

膏锋锷。

民安在?

填沟壑。

叹江山如故,

千村寥落。

何日请缨提锐旅?

一鞭直渡清河洛①。

却归来,

再续汉阳游,

骑黄鹤。

---

① 河洛:黄河、洛水一带,即指中原。

Where are our armed men?

By swords they were slain.

And people alike

Have filled moat and dyke.

Alas! The land still seems the same,

But villages lie ruined in war flame.

When can I get the order

To lead my warriors brave,

Whipping my steed, to cross the river wave

And clear the border?

When I come back, again

I'd make a Southern trip on Yellow Crane.

小重山

[宋]岳 飞

昨夜寒蛩①不住鸣,
惊回千里梦,
已三更。
起来独自绕阶行,
人悄悄,
帘外月胧明。

白首为功名,
旧山松竹老,
阻归程。
欲将心事付瑶琴②,
知音少,
弦断有谁听?

① 寒蛩(qióng):秋天的蟋蟀。
② 瑶琴:饰以美玉的琴。

Tune: Manifold Little Hill

Yue Fei

The autumn crickets chirped incessantly last night,

Breaking my dream home-bound,

'Twas already mid-night.

I got up and alone in the yard walk'd around,

On window screen the moon shone bright,

There was no human sound.

My hair turns gray

For the glorious day,

In native hills bamboos and pines grow old.

O when can I see my household?

I would confide to my lute what I have in view,

But connoisseurs are few.

Who would be listening

Though I break my lute string?

This lyric reveals implicitly the general's resentment against the capitulationists who would not sanction his resistance against the Jurchen invaders.

钗头凤[1]

[宋] 陆 游

红酥手,
黄縢[2]酒。
满城春色宫墙柳。
东风恶,
欢情薄。
一怀愁绪,
几年离索。
错,错,错!

[1] 据传唐婉曾作一首《钗头凤·世情难》相答,诗如下:世情薄,人情恶,雨送黄昏花易落。晓风干,泪痕残,欲笺心事,独语斜阑。难,难,难!人成各,今非昨,病魂常似秋千索。角声寒,夜阑珊,怕人寻问,咽泪装欢。瞒,瞒,瞒!
[2] 黄縢:宋代官酒以黄纸为封,代指美酒。

Tune: Phoenix Hairpin

Lu You

Pink hands so fine,

Gold-branded wine,

Spring paints green willows palace walls cannot confine.

East wind unfair,

Happy times rare.

In my heart sad thoughts throng:

We've severed for years long,

Wrong, wrong, wrong!

Lu You (1125—1210) was a famous patriotic poet of the Southern Song Dynasty. In the spring of 1155, he met in the Garden of Shen his first wife Tang Wan whom he loved dearly and yet from whom he was compelled to divorce.

春如旧,
人空瘦,
泪痕红浥①鲛绡②透。
桃花落,
闲池阁。
山盟虽在,
锦书难托。
莫,莫,莫!

① 浥(yì):湿润。
② 鲛绡(jiāo xiāo):神话传说鲛人所织的绡,极薄,后用以泛指薄纱,这里指手帕。

Spring is as green,

In vain she's lean,

Her silk scarf soak'd with tears and red with stains unclean.

Peach blossoms fall

Near desert'd hall.

Our oath is still there, lo!

No word to her can go.

No, no, no!

诉衷情

[宋] 陆　游

当年万里觅封侯,
匹马戍①梁州。
关河②梦断何处,
尘暗旧貂裘。

胡未灭,
鬓先秋,
泪空流。
此生谁料,
心在天山③,
身老沧洲④。

① 戍（shù）：守边。
② 关河：关塞、河流。一说指潼关黄河之所在。
③ 天山：在中国西北部，是汉唐时的边疆。这里代指南宋与金国相持的西北前线。
④ 沧洲：近水的地方，古时常用来泛指隐士居住之地。这里是指作者位于镜湖之滨的家乡。

Tune: Telling of Innermost Feelings

Lu You

Alone I went a thousand miles long, long ago
To serve the army well at the frontier.
The fortress town in dreams I could not go,
Dusty and outworn my sable-coat of cavalier.

The foe not beaten back,
My hair no longer black,
My tears have flowed in vain.
Who could have thought that in this life I would remain
With a mountain-high aim
But an old mortal frame!

In 1172 the patriotic poet served in the army stationed in Liangzhou (present-day Shaanxi Province) on the northwest frontier, with the high aim of repelling the Jurchen invasion and recovering the lost territory, but his dream was not realized even when he grew old.

卜算子

咏梅

[宋] 陆　游

驿外①断桥边,
寂寞开无主。
已是黄昏独自愁,
更著②风和雨。

无意苦③争春,
一任④群芳妒。
零落成泥碾作尘,
只有香如故。

① 驿外:指荒僻、冷清之地。驿,驿站。
② 著(zhuó):同"着",遭受,承受。
③ 苦:尽力,竭力。
④ 一任:完全听凭。

Tune: Song of Divination

Ode to the Mume Blossom

Lu You

Beside the broken bridge and outside the post-hall,
A flower is blooming forlorn.
Saddened by her solitude at night-fall,
By wind and rain she's further torn.

Let other flowers their envy pour.
To Spring she lays no claim.
Fallen in mud and ground to dust, she seems no more,
But her fragrance is still the same.

Of all the flowers the patriotic poet loved best the mume blossom, about which he wrote more than one hundred poems, for he himself felt lonely like the flower, rejected by the capitulationists in power.

念奴娇

过洞庭

[宋]张孝祥

洞庭青草,
近中秋、
更无一点风色。
玉鉴琼田三万顷,
着我扁舟一叶。
素月①分辉,
明河共影,
表里俱澄澈。
悠然心会,
妙处难与君说。

① 素月:洁白的月亮。

Tune: The Charm of A Maiden Singer

Passing Lake Dongting

Zhang Xiaoxiang

Lake Dongting, Lake Green Grass,

Near the Mid-autumn night,

Unruffled for no winds pass,

Like thirty thousand acres of jade bright

Dotted with the leaf-like boat of mine.

The skies with pure moonbeams o'erflow;

The water surface paved with moonshine:

Brightness above, brightness below.

My heart with the moon becomes one,

Felicity to share with none.

Zhang Xiaoxiang (1132—1169) was also a patriotic poet who passed the civil service examinations in 1154 with the highest honors. He was appointed governor of Jiankang (present-day Nanjing) and because he advocated the northern expedition against the Jurchen invaders, he was slandered and banished to the southwest border. This lyric was written in 1166 when, dismissed again from service, he passed Lake Dongting on his way home.

应念岭表①经年,

孤光自照,

肝胆皆冰雪。

短鬓萧疏襟袖冷,

稳泛沧溟空阔。

尽挹②西江③,

细斟北斗,

万象为宾客。

叩舷独啸,

不知今夕何夕。

① 岭表:岭外,即五岭以南的两广地区。
② 挹(yì):舀。
③ 西江:长江连通洞庭湖,中上游在洞庭以西,故称西江。

Thinking of the Southwest where I passed a year,

To lonely pure moonlight akin,

I feel my heart and soul snow-and-ice-clear.

Although my hair is short and sparse, my gown too thin,

In the immense expanse I keep floating up.

Drinking wine from the River West

And using Dipper as a wine-cup,

I invite Nature to be my guest.

Beating time aboard and crooning alone,

I sink deep into time and place unknown.

西江月

[宋]张孝祥

问讯湖①边春色,
重来又是三年。
东风吹我过湖船,
杨柳丝丝拂面。

世路如今已惯,
此心到处悠然。
寒光亭②下水如天,
飞起沙鸥一片。

① 湖:指三塔湖。
② 寒光亭:在三塔寺内。

Tune: The Moon over the West River

Zhang Xiaoxiang

Does the lakeside spring scene the same remain?
Three years have passed now that I come again.
Across the surface of the lake the east wind blows my boat,
The willow branches wreath by wreath caress my face and coat.

I'm used to life both high and low,
My heart's at ease where'er I go.
Water looks like the sky below Bower Cold-light,
It's ruffled only by the waterbirds in flight.

This lyric describes a lake scene in the South and expresses the poet's feeling after his dismissal from civil service.

水龙吟

登建康①赏心亭

[宋] 辛弃疾

楚天千里清秋,

水随天去秋无际。

遥岑②远目,

献愁供恨,

玉簪螺髻。

落日楼头,

断鸿声里,

江南游子。

把吴钩③看了,

阑干拍遍,

无人会、

登临意。

---

① 建康:今江苏南京。
② 遥岑(cén):远山。
③ 吴钩:古代吴地制造的一种宝刀。

Tune: Water Dragon Chant

On Riverside Tower at Jiankang

Xin Qiji

The Southern sky for miles and miles in autumn dye,

And boundless autumn water spread to meet the sky,

I gaze on far-off Northern hills

Like spiral shells or hair decor of jade

Which grief or hatred overfills.

Leaning at sunset on balustrade

And hearing a lonely swan's song,

A wanderer on Southern land,

I look at my precious sword long

And pound all the railings with my hand,

But nobody knows why

I climb the tower high.

Xin Qiji (1140—1207) was regarded as the greatest lyric poet of the Southern Song Dynasty and a patriotic poet par excellence. At the age of twenty-two, he fought against the Jurchen invaders overrunning his native land in the North. This lyric was written in 1167 when the poet, coming to the South, served as a petty official in Jiankang (present-day Nanjing). One autumn day, ascending the Riverside Tower on the Western City Gate and seeing the hills on the Northern shore, he sighed for he could not wield his sword to fight against the foe and recapture the lost land in the North.

休说鲈鱼堪脍,

尽西风、

季鹰归未?

求田问舍,

怕应羞见、

刘郎才气。

可惜流年,

忧愁风雨,

树犹如此。

倩①何人、

唤取红巾翠袖②,

揾③英雄泪。

① 倩(qìng):请托。
② 红巾翠袖:女子装饰,代指女子。
③ 揾(wèn):擦拭。

Don't say for food

The perch is good.

When the west winds blow,

Why don't I homeward go?

I'd be ashamed to see the patriot,

Should I retire to seek for land and cot.

I sigh for passing years I can't retain,

In driving wind and blinding rain

Even an old tree grieves.

To whom then may I say

To wipe my tears away

With her pink handkerchief or her green sleeves?

菩萨蛮

书江西造口壁

[宋]辛弃疾

郁孤台①下清江水,
中间多少行人②泪。
西北望长安③,
可怜无数山。

青山遮不住,
毕竟东流去。
江晚正愁余④,
山深闻鹧鸪⑤。

---

① 郁孤台:《赣州府志》记载:"郁孤台,一名贺兰山,隆阜郁然孤山峙,故名。唐李勉为刺史,登台北望,慨然曰:'予虽不及子牟,心在魏阙一也,郁孤岂令乎?'乃易匾为'望阙'。"
② 行人:指逃难的人。
③ 长安:代指京城汴梁,李白《登金陵凤凰台》有"总为浮云能蔽日,长安不见使人愁"之句。
④ 余:我。
⑤ 鹧鸪:鸟名,其声音像"行不得也哥哥"。听这种声音容易触动羁旅之愁。

Tune: Buddhist Dancers

Written on the Wall at Zaokou, Jiangxi

Xin Qiji

Below the Gloomy Terrace flow two rivers clear,

The tears of refugees were shed when they were here!

I gaze afar on land long lost in the northwest,

Alas! I see but hill on hill and crest on crest.

But blue hills can't stop water flowing,

Eastward the river keeps on going.

At dusk the river grieves me still,

The partridges call in the hill.

In 1129, the Jurchen invaders drove southward as far as Zaokou, Jiangxi, and massacred many refugees near the Gloomy Terrace in Ganzhou where united Rivers Zhang and Gong. In 1176, the poet passing by Zaokou was grieved at the sight of the tearful river and at the call of the partridge which seemed to say in Chinese: "Why not go home?"

摸鱼儿

[宋] 辛弃疾

> 淳熙己亥①,自湖北漕②移湖南,同官王正之置酒小山亭,为赋。

更能消几番风雨,

匆匆春又归去。

惜春长怕花开早,

何况落红无数。

春且住,

见说道③、

天涯芳草无归路。

怨春不语。

算只有殷勤、

画檐蛛网,

尽日惹飞絮。

① 淳熙己亥:宋孝宗淳熙六年(1179)。
② 湖北漕:荆湖北路掌管钱粮的转运副使。漕,转运使的简称。
③ 见说道:听说。

Tune: Groping for Fish

Xin Qiji

> In 1179, before I was transferred from Hubei to Hunan, Wang Chengzhi, a colleague of mine, feasted me in the Little Hill Pavilion and I wrote the following lyric.

How much more can Spring bear of wind and rain?

Too hastily, I fear, 'twill leave again.

Lovers of Spring would fear to see the flowers red

Budding too soon and fallen petals too wide spread

O Spring, please stay!

I've heard it said that sweet grass far away

Would stop you from seeing your backward way.

But I've not heard

Spring say a word,

Only the busy spiders weave

Webs all day by the painted eave

To keep the willow-down from taking leave.

In the first stanza the patriotic poet sighed for the departing spring, for he could not do what he wanted, that is, drive away Jurchen invaders from the occupied territory. In the second stanza he compared himself to a disfavored Beauty and the capitulationists to the plump and slender dancers in favor. The willow trees were heartbroken for they often saw people part.

长门①事，

准拟佳期又误。

蛾眉曾有人妒。

千金纵买相如赋，

脉脉此情谁诉？

君莫舞，

君不见、

玉环飞燕②皆尘土。

闲愁最苦。

休去倚危栏，

斜阳正在、

烟柳断肠处。

① 长门：汉代宫名。汉武帝之陈皇后，失宠住在长门宫。曾送黄金百斤给司马相如，请他代写一篇赋送给汉武帝，陈皇后因而重新得宠。后世遂把"长门"作为失宠后妃居处的专用名词。
② 玉环飞燕：杨玉环，唐玄宗的爱妃，后被赐死。赵飞燕，汉成帝的皇后，后自杀。两人都得宠且善嫉妒。

Could a disfavored consort again to favor rise?

Could Beauty not be envied by green eyes?

Even if favor could be bought back again,

To whom of this unanswered love can she complain?

Do not dance then!

Have you not seen

Both plump and slender beauties turn to dust?

Bitterest grief is just

That you can't do

What you want to.

O! Do not lean

On overhanging rails where the setting sun sees

Heart-broken willow trees!

清平乐

独宿博山[1]王氏庵[2]

[宋] 辛弃疾

绕床饥鼠,
蝙蝠翻灯舞。
屋上松风吹急雨,
破纸窗间自语。

平生塞北江南,
归来华发苍颜。
布被秋宵梦觉,
眼前万里江山。

[1] 博山: 在今江西省上饶市。
[2] 王氏庵: 王氏人家的草屋。

Tune: Pure Serene Music

Passing One Lonely Night at Boshan

Xin Qiji

Around the bed run hungry rats,
In lamplight to and fro fly bats.
On pine-shad'd roof the wind and shower rattle,
The window paper-scraps are heard to prattle.

I roam from north to south, from place to place,
And come back with gray hair and wrinkled face.
I woke up in thin quilt on autumn night.
The boundless land I dreamed of still remains in sight.

Unable to do what he wanted to, the patriotic poet lived in the countryside of Jiangxi. This lyric described one lonely night he passed in a convent at Boshan and his dream of the lost land.

清平乐

村居

[宋] 辛弃疾

茅檐①低小,
溪上青青草。
醉里吴音②相媚好,
白发谁家翁媪③。
大儿锄豆④溪东,
中儿正织鸡笼;
最喜小儿无赖,
溪头卧剥莲蓬。

① 茅檐:茅屋的屋檐。
② 吴音:吴地的方言。
③ 翁媪(ǎo):老翁、老妇。
④ 锄豆:锄掉豆田里的草。

Tune: Pure Serene Music

Rural Life

Xin Qiji

The thatched roof is slanting low,

Beside the brook green grasses grow.

Who talks with drunken. Southern voice so sweet?

A white-haired man and wife in their retreat.

East of the brook their eldest son is hoeing weeds;

Their second son now makes a cage for hens he feeds.

I like their youngest son who, having nothing done,

Lies by the brook podding lotus seeds one by one.

This lyric depicts a happy family of Southern villagers.

采桑子

[宋] 辛弃疾

少年不识愁滋味,
爱上层楼,
爱上层楼,
为赋新词强说愁①。

而今识尽愁滋味,
欲说还休②,
欲说还休,
却道天凉好个秋!

---

① 强说愁:无愁而勉强说愁。
② 欲说还休:李清照《凤凰台上忆吹箫》有"多少事,欲说还休"。

Tune: Song of Picking Mulberry

Xin Qiji

While young, I knew no grief I could not bear,
I'd like to go upstair.
I'd like to go upstair
To write new verses, with a false despair.

I know what grief is now that I am old,
I would not have it told.
I would not have it told
But only say I'm glad that autumn's cold.

Thins lyric reveals implicitly the poet's grief of being unable to fulfil his ambition.

青玉案

元夕①

[宋] 辛弃疾

东风夜放花千树,
更吹落、星如雨。
宝马雕车香满路。
凤箫声动,
玉壶光转,
一夜鱼龙舞②。

蛾儿雪柳黄金缕,
笑语盈盈暗香去。
众里寻他千百度,
蓦然③回首,
那人却在、
灯火阑珊④处。

① 元夕:即元宵节,此夜称元夕或元夜。
② 鱼龙舞:指舞动鱼形、龙形的彩灯,如鱼龙闹海一样。
③ 蓦(mò)然:突然,猛然。
④ 阑珊:零落稀疏的样子。

Tune: Green Jade Cup

Lantern Festival

Xin Qiji

One night's east wind adorns a thousand trees with flowers

And blows down stars in showers.

Fine steeds and carved cabs spread fragrance en route,

Music vibrates from the flute,

The moon sheds its full light

While fish and dragon lanterns dance all night.

In gold-thread dress, with moth or willow ornaments,

Giggling, they melt into the throng with trails of scents.

But in the crowd once and again

I look for her in vain.

When all at once I turn my head,

I find her there where lantern light is dimly shed.

The Lantern Festival was the 15th day of the 1st lunar month when Chinese people used to adorn trees with lanterns as if they were stars falling in showers to vie in brightness with the full moon. In this lyric the poet contrasted the lady he was looking for with the throng of golden-dressed women so as to show her and his lofty character.

破阵子

为陈同甫赋壮词以寄之

[宋] 辛弃疾

醉里挑灯看剑,
梦回吹角连营。
八百里[①]分麾[②]下炙,
五十弦[③]翻塞外声。
沙场秋点兵。

马作的卢飞快,
弓如霹雳弦惊。
了却君王天下事,
赢得生前身后名。
可怜白发生。

---

① 八百里:指牛,泛指酒食。
② 麾:军旗。麾下:指部下。
③ 五十弦:本指瑟,泛指乐器。

Tune: Dance of the Cavalry

Written for Chen Liang

Xin Qiji

Drunken, I lit my lamp to see my glaive,

Awake, I heard the horns from tents to tents

Under the flags, beef grilled

Was eaten by our warriors brave

And martial airs were played by fifty instruments:

'Twas an autumn manoeuvre in the field.

On gallant steed

Running full speed,

We'd shoot with twanging bows.

Recovering the lost land for the sovereign,

'Tis everlasting fame that we would win.

But alas! white hair grows!

In this lyric written for his friend Chen Liang who visited him in 1143, the poet recollected their life in the anti-Jurchen army, encouraged his younger friend to fight against the foe and regretted that he himself was growing old.

西江月

夜行黄沙道中

[宋] 辛弃疾

明月别枝惊鹊,
清风半夜鸣蝉。
稻花香里说丰年,
听取蛙声一片。

七八个星天外,
两三点雨山前。
旧时茅店①社林②边,
路转溪桥忽见。

① 茅店:茅草盖的乡村客店。
② 社林:土地庙附近的树林。

Tune: The Moon over the West River

A Summer Night on My Way Home from the Yellow Sand Ridge

Xin Qiji

Startled by magpies leaving the branch in moonlight;
I hear cicadas shrill in the breeze at midnight.
The ricefields' sweet smell promises a harvest great,
I listen to the frogs' croak when the night grows late.

Beyond the clouds seven or eight stars twinkle;
Before the hills two or three raindrops sprinkle.
There is an inn beside the Village Temple. Look!
The winding path leads to the hut beside the brook.

The Yellow Sand Ridge was situated to the west of Shangrao, Jiangxi, where the poet lived when he could not fulfil his ambition to fight against the Jurchen aggressors. This lyric depicts a nocturnal journey of the poet who was startled and surprised to see magpies leaving the branch in moonlight and glad to smell the sweet smell of the ricefields and to hear the frogs croak which announced a good harvest, and then again surprised by the coming rain and glad to find an inn by the side of the brook.

西江月

遣兴

[宋] 辛弃疾

醉里且①贪欢笑,
要愁那得工夫。
近来始觉古人书,
信着全无是处。

昨夜松边醉倒,
问松我醉何如?
只疑松动要来扶,
以手推松曰去。

① 且:犹,还。

Tune: The Moon over the West River

Written at Random

Xin Qiji

Drunken, I'll laugh my fill,
Having no time to be grieved.
Books of the ancients may say what they will,
They cannot be wholly believed.

Drunken last night beneath a pine-tree,
I asked it if it liked me so drunk.
Afraid it would bend to try to raise me,
"Be off!" I said and pushed back its trunk.

This is a vivid portrayal of the drunken poet who was grieved that the books of the ancient sages became useless now that what they said could no longer be put into practice, which reveals the poet's discontent with the situation of the Southern Song Dynasty. In the last line the poet injects an extremely colloquial expression borrowed from ancient prose classics.

鹧鸪天

[宋] 辛弃疾

有客慨然谈功名，因追念少年时事，戏作。

壮岁旌旗拥万夫，
锦襜突骑①渡江初。
燕兵夜娖②银胡䩮③，
汉箭朝飞金仆姑。

追往事，
叹今吾，
春风不染白髭须④。
却将万字平戎策，
换得东家⑤种树书⑥。

① 锦襜（chān）突骑：穿锦绣短衣的快速骑兵。襜，战袍。
② 娖（chuò）：整理。
③ 银胡䩮（lù）：银色或镶银的箭袋。
④ 髭（zī）须：胡子。唇上为"髭"，唇下为"须"。
⑤ 东家：东邻。
⑥ 种树书：研究栽培树木的书。此喻退休归耕农田。

Tune: The Partridge Sky

Xin Qiji

> As a friend of mine talked about the victory we had won while young, I recollected those bygone days and wrote the following random lyric.

While young, beneath my flag I had ten thousand knights,

With these outfitted cavaliers I crossed the River.

The foe prepared their silver shafts during the nights;

During the days we shot darts from golden quiver.

Recalling days gone by,

I sigh over my plight:

The vernal wind can't change my hair to black from white.

Since thwarted is my plan for gaining the lost land,

I'd learn from gentle neighbors how to plant fruit trees by hand.

In 1162, Xin Qiji aged twenty-three captured the traitor who had assassinated the leader of the Anti-Jurchen forces in the North, led his troops across the Yangzi River and served in the court of Southern Song. But his plan for taking back the lost Northern land was not adopted and he could not but live in seclusion in the countryside and learn from his neighbours how to cultivate the land.

永遇乐

京口北固亭[①]怀古

[宋] 辛弃疾

千古江山,

英雄无觅,

孙仲谋处。

舞榭[②]歌台,

风流总被,

雨打风吹去。

斜阳草树,

寻常巷陌,

人道寄奴[③]曾住。

想当年,

金戈铁马,

气吞万里如虎。

---

① 北固亭:在今江苏省镇江市北固山上,下临长江,三面环水。
② 榭(xiè):建在高台上的房子。
③ 寄奴:南朝宋武帝刘裕小名。

Tune: Joy of Eternal Union

Thinking of Ancient Heroes in the Tower on the Northern Hill at Jingkou

Xin Qiji

The land is boundless as of yore,

But nowhere can be found

A hero like the King defending Southern shore.

The singing hall, the dancing ground,

All gallant deeds now sent away

By driving wind and blinding rain.

The slanting sun sheds its departing ray

O'er country tree-shaded and grassy lane

Where lived the Cowherd King retaking the lost land.

In bygone years,

Leading armed cavaliers,

With golden spear in hand,

Tiger-like, he had slain

The foe on the thousand-mile Central Plain.

In 1204, the sixty-six years old poet was appointed governor of Jingkou (present-day Zhengjiang, Jiangsu Province) and wrote this lyric. The King defending the Southern shore alludes to Sun Quan (Sun Zhongmou) who defeated the Northern forces at the Red Cliff in AD 208. The Cowherd-King alludes to Liu Yu (reigned 420—422) who was born in Jingkou and who won great victory over the Northern invaders occupying the Central Plain. The thriving town refers to Yangzhou destroyed by the Jurchen aggressors in 1162 and the old general to the sixty-six years old governor himself.

元嘉草草①,

封狼居胥②,

赢得仓皇北顾。

四十三年,

望中犹记,

烽火扬州路③。

可堪回首,

佛狸祠④下,

一片神鸦社鼓⑤。

凭谁问,

廉颇老矣,

尚能饭否?

---

① 元嘉:刘义隆年号。
② 封狼居胥:狼居胥山,在内蒙古自治区西北部。
③ 烽火扬州路:当年扬州地区到处都是抗击金兵南侵的痕迹。
④ 佛(bì)狸祠:拓跋焘小名佛狸。元嘉二十七年(450年),拓跋焘反击刘宋,两个月时间里,从黄河北岸一路穿插到长江北岸,在长江北岸瓜步山建立行宫,即后来的佛狸祠。
⑤ 神鸦:在庙里吃祭品的乌鸦。社鼓:祭祀时的鼓声。

His son launched in haste a Northern campaign,

Defeated at Mount Wolf, he shed his tears in vain.

I still remember three and forty years ago

The thriving town destroyed in the flames by the foe.

How can I bear

To see the chief aggressor's shrine

Worshipped 'mid crows and drum-beats as divine?

Who would still care

If an old general

Is strong enough to take back the lost capital?

南乡子

登京口北固亭有怀

[宋] 辛弃疾

何处望神州?
满眼风光北固楼。
千古兴亡多少事,
悠悠。
不尽长江滚滚流。

年少万兜鍪①,
坐断②东南战未休。
天下英雄谁敌手?
曹刘。
生子当如孙仲谋。

① 兜鍪(móu):原指古代作战时兵士所戴的头盔,这里代指士兵。
② 坐断:坐镇,割据。

Tune: Song of a Southern Country

Reflections on Ascending the Tower on the Northern Hill at Jingkou

Xin Qiji

Where is the Central Plain?
I gaze beyond the Northern Tower in vain.
It has seen dynasties fall and rise
As time flies
Or as the endless River rolls before my eyes.

While young Sun had ten thousand men at his command,
Steeled in battles, he defend'd the southeastern land.
Among his equals in the world, who were heroes true
But Cao and Liu?
And even Cao would have a son like Sun Zhongmou.

This is another lyric written by the old governor of Jingkou who ascended the Northern Tower overlooking the Yangzi River and gazed from afar on the lost Central Plain beyond the Northern shore. Sun (Sun Quan or Sun Zhongmou), Cao (Cao Cao) and Liu (Liu Bei) were three kings of the Three Kingdoms Period (220—280).

水调歌头
送章德茂大卿使虏

[宋] 陈 亮

不见南师久,
漫说北群空①。
当场只手②,
毕竟还我万夫雄。
自笑堂堂汉使,
得似③洋洋河水,
依旧只流东。
且复穹庐拜,
会向藁街④逢。

---

① 北群空:指有才干的人被选拔走。韩愈《送温处士赴河阳军序》有:"伯乐一过冀北之野,而群马遂空。"
② 只手:指独当一面。
③ 得似:难道像。
④ 藁街:汉代长安街名,外族使臣居住的地方。

Tune: Prelude to Water Melody

Farewell to Zhang Demao, Envoy to Jurchen Aggressors

Chen Liang

Not seeing Southern troops for long,

Don't say the Northern steeds can't run.

Single-handed, at once the thing is done,

After all, we are heroes millions strong.

His Majesty's Envoy—what fun!

Should eastwards go like overbrimming River

Which eastwards flows forever.

We bend to the Jurchen tents now,

Another day to us they'll bow.

Chen Liang (1143—1194) was a patriotic poet and a friend of Xin Qiji's, Zhang Demao was His Majesty's Envoy sent single-handed to bow to the Jurchen chieftain who was accustomed to mutton-eating. The Northern steeds refer to those of the Southern troops and the sun to the Song Empire.

尧之都,

舜之壤,

禹之封,

于中应有、

一个半个耻臣戎①。

万里腥膻②如许,

千古英灵安在,

磅礴几时通?

胡运何须问,

赫日③自当中。

---

① 戎:古代对少数民族的蔑称。
② 腥膻(shān):指羊的腥臊气,指中原被金人盘踞。
③ 赫日:烈日。

In the capital of one emperor

And the land of another great, long

Empire built by our ancestor,

Is there none who thinks it wrong

To submit to the foe

Whose stink of mutton spreads for miles and miles?

Where's the spirit of heroes who died long ago?

When will our army beat the Jurchen ranks and files?

Why ask about the enemy's fate?

The sun will surely radiate.

西江月

[宋] 刘 过

堂上谋臣帷幄①,
边头猛将干戈②。
天时地利与人和,
燕可伐欤曰:"可可"。

此日楼台鼎鼐③,
他时剑履山河。
都人齐和大风歌④,
管领群臣来贺。

① 帷幄:本指帐幕,这里指谋国之心。
② 干戈:古代的两种武器,这里比喻战争。
③ 鼎鼐(nài):古代的烹调用具,古时常用鼎鼐调味来比喻宰相的职责或者指治国。
④ 大风歌:刘邦曾有《大风歌》一诗:"大风起兮云飞扬,威加海内兮归故乡,安得猛士兮守四方。"

Tune: The Moon over the West River

Liu Guo

Ministers in the court plan the campaign;

Generals spear in hand guard the frontier.

When can we take back the lost Central Plain?

Our men, united, should start now and here.

Holding the premiership today,

You'll win high honor tomorrow.

The capital retaken, you may sing the lay

Of Big Wind and people will follow.

Liu Guo (1154—1206) was a patriotic poet and a follower of Xin Qiji. This lyric was written for Premier Han who planned a Northern campaign to take back the lost Central Plain and the lost capital. The Song of the Great Wind was a song written by the first Emperor of the Han Dynasty (reigned 206—194 BC), which reads as follows:
The big wind rises and drives clouds away,
I come home now that I hold the world under sway.
Where are my brave men to guard the frontiers today?

扬州慢

[宋] 姜 夔

淳熙丙申至日,余过维扬。夜雪初霁,荠麦弥望。入其城,则四顾萧条,寒水自碧,暮色渐起,戍角悲吟。余怀怆然,感慨今昔。因自度此曲。千岩老人以为有黍离之悲也。

淮左①名都,

竹西②佳处,

解鞍少驻初程。

过春风十里③,

尽荠麦青青。

自胡马窥江④去后,

废池乔木,

犹厌言兵。

渐黄昏,清角吹寒,

都在空城。

① 淮左:宋在苏北和江淮设淮南东路和淮南西路,淮南东路又称淮左。
② 竹西:扬州城东一亭名,景色清幽。
③ 春风十里:借指昔日扬州的最繁华处。
④ 胡马窥江:1129年和1161年,金兵两次南下,扬州都遭到惨重破坏。

Tune: Slow Tune of Yangzhou

Jiang Kui

On Winter Solstice in 1127, I passed Yangzhou. It turned fine after one night of snow. I saw the fields overgrown with wild wheat and weeds. When I entered the ruined town, I looked around and was grieved to see green water cold and to hear sad horns blow at dusk. I felt sad and dreary to compare the present desolation with the past glory and composed the following tune which reveals the grief of a ruined country, as says my old uncle-in-law.

In the famous town east of River Huai

And scenic spot of Bamboo West,

Breaking my journey, I alight for a short rest.

In breeze the splendid three-mile road did I pass by.

'Tis now o'ergrown with wild green wheat and weeds.

Since Southern shore was overrun by Jurchen steeds,

E'en the tall trees beside the pond have been war-torn.

As dusk is drawing near,

Cold blows the horn,

The empty town looks drear.

Jiang Kui (1155?—1221) was the first musician among the lyrical poets of the Southern Song Dynasty. This lyric was written when he passed by Yangzhou, most prosperous city before Jurchen invasion, situated to the east of the River Huai and well known for scenic spots such as the Pavilion of West Bamboo and Twenty-four Bridges.

杜郎①俊赏,
算而今、
重到须惊。
纵豆蔻②词工,
青楼梦③好,
难赋深情。
二十四桥④仍在,
波心荡、冷月无声。
念桥边红药⑤,
年年知为谁生。

① 杜郎:唐朝诗人杜牧,他在扬州以诗酒清狂著称。
② 豆蔻(kòu):本是一种植物,二月初刚发芽,后常常用来指柔弱美丽的十三四岁的少女。
③ 青楼梦:出自杜牧《遣怀》:"十年一觉扬州梦,赢得青楼薄幸名。"
④ 二十四桥:在扬州西郊,传说有二十四美人吹箫于此。
⑤ 桥边红药:二十四桥又名红药桥,桥边生红芍药。

The place Du Mu the poet prized,
If he could come again today,
Would make him feel surprised.
His verse on the cardamon spray
And on sweet dreams in Mansions Green
Could not express
My deep distress.
The Twenty-four Bridges can still be seen,
But the cold moon floating among
The waves would no more sing a song.
For whom should the peonies near
The Bridges grow red from year to year?

鹧鸪天

元夕有所梦

[宋]姜　夔

肥水①东流无尽期，
当初不合种相思。
梦中未比丹青见，
暗里忽惊山鸟啼。

春未绿，
鬓先丝，
人间别久不成悲。
谁教岁岁红莲②夜，
两处沉吟各自知。

① 肥水：指东肥河，出自合肥西北将军岭，宋时流入巢湖。
② 红莲：指灯笼，欧阳修《元夕词》中有："纤手染香罗，剪红莲满城开遍。"

Tune: The Partridge Sky

A Dream on the Night of Lantern Festival

Jiang Kui

The long River Fei to the east keeps on flowing;

The love-seeds we once sowed forever keep growing.

Your face I saw in dreams was not clear to my eyes

As in your portrait, soon I'm woke up by birds' cries.

Spring not yet green,

My gray hair seen,

Our separation has been too long to grieve the heart.

Who makes the past reappear

Before us from year to year

On Lantern Festival when we are far apart?

This is a love lyric written on the 15th day of the first lunar month in 1197. The over-forty-year-old poet dreamed of his beloved from whom he had been separated for more than twenty years.

玉楼春

戏林推

[宋] 刘克庄

年年跃马长安①市,
客舍似家家似寄②。
青钱③换酒日无何④,
红烛呼卢⑤宵不寐。

易挑锦妇机中字⑥,
难得玉人⑦心下事。
男儿西北有神州,
莫滴水西桥⑧畔泪。

① 长安:这里借指南宋都城临安。
② 寄:客居。
③ 青钱:古铜钱成色不同,分青钱、黄钱两种。
④ 无何:不过问其他的事情。
⑤ 红烛呼卢:晚上点蜡烛赌博。
⑥ 机中字:织锦中的文字。
⑦ 玉人:美人,这里指歌伎。这句说妓女的心事是不易捉摸的。
⑧ 水西桥:泛指歌伎所居之地,这句说不要为妓女浪费自己的眼泪。

Tune: Spring in Jade Pavilion

Written in Jest for a Friend

Liu Kezhuang

You gallop in the capital year after year,

More than at home in brothels you appear.

You spend your coins on wine, washing your day;

By candlelight you gamble all the night away.

Why should you abandon your wife faithful to you?

Don't you know a fair mistress's heart won't be true?

A gallant man should not forget lost northwest lands.

Do not shed tears where your mistress's mansion stands!

Liu Kezhuang (1187—1269) was a patriotic poet of the Southern Song Dynasty. This lyric was advice to one of his friends.

八声甘州

陪庾幕[①]诸公游灵岩[②]

[宋] 吴文英

渺空烟四远。

是何年、

青天坠长星?

幻苍崖云树,

名娃[③]金屋,

残霸[④]宫城。

箭径酸风射眼,

腻水[⑤]染花腥。

时靸[⑥]双鸳响,

廊叶秋声。

① 庾(yǔ)幕:指提举常平仓的官衙中的幕友西宾。
② 灵岩:又名石鼓山,在苏州市西南的木渎镇西北。
③ 名娃:指西施。
④ 残霸:指吴王夫差。
⑤ 腻水:宫女灌妆的脂粉水。
⑥ 靸(sǎ):一种草制的拖鞋。此作穿着拖鞋。

Tune: Eight Beats of a Ganzhou Song

Visiting the Star Cliff with My Friends

Wu Wenying

Mist spreads as far as sees the eye.

When did this big star fall from the blue sky?

It changed to a green cliff with cloud-like trees,

With golden bowers built for lady fair

In Wu's great palace, now in sad debris.

On Arrow Lane the eyes were hurt in chilly air,

And rouged water stained with fallen flowers sweet.

Leaves fall on hollow ground,

'Tis Autumn's sound,

It seems as if I heard the lady's slippered feet.

The Star Cliff is situated in the west of Suzhou, capital of the ancient Kingdom of Wu. The king of Wu built a palace on the Cliff with a golden bower for his favourite mistress Xi Shi and drank with her in the Gallery of Hollow Ground, beside the Arrow Lane or on the Lute Terrace. At last his kingdom was conquered by the king of Yue and General Fan Li who, after the conquest of Wu, retreated as a hermit to the lakeside and lived together with the beautiful lady Xi Shi.

宫里吴王沉醉。
倩五湖倦客[①],
独钓醒醒。
问苍天无语,
华发奈山青。
水涵空,
阑干高处,
送乱鸦斜日落渔汀[②]。
连呼酒,
上琴台[③]去,
秋与云平。

① 五湖倦客:指范蠡。
② 渔汀:水边捕鱼处。
③ 琴台:春秋时期吴王游乐的遗迹,在灵岩山上。

In Wu's great palace, drunk the king did lie,
But the tired hermit on the lake
Fished all alone awake.
In vain I ask the silent sky,
My hair turns gray in face of mountains green.
The sky in water mirrored seen,
Leaning on railings high,
I see crows scatter on the beach in setting sun.
I ask for wine both long and loud,
And stand upon Lute Terrace where is none
But autumn high and lonely as the cloud.

风入松

[宋] 吴文英

听风听雨过清明,
愁草①瘗②花铭。
楼前绿暗分携路,
一丝柳、一寸柔情。
料峭春寒中酒③,
交加晓梦啼莺。

西园日日扫林亭,
依旧赏新晴。
黄蜂频扑秋千索,
有当时纤手香凝。
惆怅双鸳不到,
幽阶一夜苔生。

① 愁草:没有心情写。
② 瘗(yì):埋葬。
③ 中(zhòng)酒:醉酒。

Tune: Wind through Pines

Wu Wenying

Hearing the wind and rain while mourning for the dead,
Sadly I draft an elegy on flowers.
We parted on the dark-green road before these bowers,
Where willow branches hang like thread,
Each inch revealing
Our tender feeling.
I drown my grief in wine in chilly spring,
Drowsy, I wake again when orioles sing.

In Garden West I sweep the pathway
From day to day,
Enjoying the fine view
Still without you.
On the ropes of the swing the wasps often alight
For fragrance spread by fingers fair.
I'm grieved not to see your foot-traces: all night
The mossy steps are left untrodden there.

On the day of mourning for the dead in chilly spring, the poet was yearning for his beloved with whom he had parted on the willow-shaded lane. Saddened, he buried fallen flowers and wrote an elegy on them. In vain he tried to drown his sorrow in wine and in sleep. In vain he swept the pathway, waiting for her arrival. He was further grieved at the sight of the swing on which he had seen her sitting and of the mossy steps which still bore the traces of her feet.

柳梢青

[宋] 刘辰翁

铁马蒙毡①,
银花②洒泪,
春入愁城③。
笛里番腔④,
街头戏鼓⑤,
不是歌声⑥。

那堪独坐青灯。
想故国、
高台月明。
辇下⑦风光,
山中岁月,
海上心情。

① 铁马:指代元军。蒙毡:披着毛毡。
② 银花:指元宵花灯。这句是说亡国后看上元灯市,灯烛好像也伴人洒泪。
③ 愁城:被元军占领的故都临安。
④ 番腔:蒙古人吹唱的腔调。
⑤ 戏鼓:指蒙古族的鼓吹杂戏。
⑥ 不是歌声:不成腔调,含有鄙夷和怀旧的意思。
⑦ 辇下:皇帝脚下,指临安城。

Tune: Green Tip of Willow Branch

Liu Chenweng

Tartarian steeds in blanket clad,
Tears shed from lanterns 'neath the moon,
Spring has come to a town so sad.
The flutes playing a foreign tune
And foreign drum-beats in the street
Can never be called music sweet.

How can I bear to sit alone by dim lamplight,
Thinking of Northern land now lost to sight
With palaces steeped in moonlight;
Of Southern capital in days gone by;
Of my secluded life in mountains high;
Of grief of those who seawards fly!

Liu Chenweng (1231—1294) was a patriotic poet of the Southern Song Dynasty. The first stanza of this lyric depicts a Lantern Festival in Linan (present-day Hangzhou), capital of Southern Song occupied by the Tartars in 1276. In the second stanza, the poet reveals his feeling towards the lost Northern land, the occupied Southern capital and the remnant of unyielding Song forces still carrying on an armed resistance on the sea.

念奴娇

驿中言别友人[①]

[宋] 文天祥

水天空阔,

恨东风、

不借[②]世间英物。

蜀鸟[③]吴花[④]残照里,

忍见荒城颓壁。

铜雀春情[⑤],

金人[⑥]秋泪,

此恨凭谁雪。

堂堂剑气,

斗牛空认奇杰。

[①] 驿中言别友人:金陵驿馆送别友人。
[②] 不借:不助。
[③] 蜀鸟:指鸣声凄怨的子规鸟,也称杜鹃鸟。
[④] 吴花:指金陵的花。
[⑤] 铜雀春情:铜雀指曹操建造的铜雀台。杜牧《赤壁》:"东风不与周郎便,铜雀春深锁二乔。"文天祥借这个典故,暗指的是宋朝投降以后所有的嫔妃都归于元宫了。
[⑥] 金人:汉武帝时铸造的捧露盘的仙人。

Tune: Charm of a Maiden Singer

Farewell to a Friend at Post House

Wen Tianxiang

The water's boundless like the skies,

But favourable wind won't rise,

To our regret, to help our heroes on the earth.

The cuckoo cries

'Mid Southern flowers in setting sun.

How could I bear to see the ruined town o'errun

By the Tartarian foe!

The captives have no mirth,

E'en golden statues that should hear

The story would drop tear on tear.

Who would not strike a vengeful blow?

The sword once shed a vengeful light,

But, swordsman beaten, when would it again shine bright?

Wen Tianxiang (1236—1282) passed the civil service examinations with the highest honour in 1256 and was appointed prime minister in the court of Song Dynasty.

那信①江海余生,

南行万里,

属扁舟齐发。

正为鸥盟留醉眼,

细看涛生云灭。

睨柱吞嬴,

回旗走懿②,

千古冲冠发。

伴人无寐,

秦淮应是孤月。

---

① 那信:想不到。
② 睨(nì)柱吞嬴,回旗走懿:指蔺相如气势压倒秦王和诸葛亮死后仍令司马懿丧胆。

Who would believe, confiding our lives to a boat,

Together we could keep afloat

On river and on sea,

Sailing southward for miles then at last we were free!

We made our plan with our allies

To wait with drunken eyes

For waves and clouds dark to appear

And disappear.

Against the chieftain of the foe,

I would fight in weal and in woe.

Wrath sets my hair on end

And it will never die.

Sleepless at night, you would only have for friend

The lonely moon on the River Qinhuai.

沁园春

题潮阳张许二公庙[①]

[宋] 文天祥

为子死孝,
为臣死忠,
死又何妨。
自光岳气分,
士无全节;
君臣义缺,
谁负刚肠。
骂贼张巡,
爱君许远,
留取声名万古香。
后来者,
无二公之操,
百炼之钢。

① 潮阳:今广东省汕头市潮阳区西北。张许二公:张巡,许远,唐代爱国将领。

人生翕欻①云亡。

好烈烈轰轰做一场。

使当时卖国,

甘心降虏,

受人唾骂,

安得留芳。

古庙幽沉,

仪容俨雅②,

枯木寒鸦几夕阳。

邮亭③下,

有奸雄过此,

仔细思量。

① 翕(xī)欻(xū):倏忽,闪动貌。
② 仪容:指张、许两人的塑像。俨雅:庄严典雅。
③ 邮亭:古代设在沿途、供给公家送文书及旅客歇宿的馆舍。

Tune: Spring in the Garden of Qin

Written in the Temples of Their Excellencies Zhang Xun and Xu Yuan

Wen Tianxiang

If sons should die for filial piety

And ministers for loyalty,

What matters for us to be dead?

Our sacred land is torn to shred,

No patriot could feel at ease,

No Loyal subject has done what he ought to do.

What could my righteous wrath appease?

Zhang Xun whom the rebels could not subdue

And Xu Yuan were loyal to the crown,

They have left an undying renown.

Those who come after them would feel

The lack of their own loyal zeal

And like them should be hardened into steel.

This lyric was written at Chaoyang when the poet passed by the Temple of General Zhang Xun and Governor Xu Yuan of the Tang Dynasty, who would not submit the city to the besieging rebels and sacrificed their lives after the fall of the city.